Eldritch Beasts

Book 5

The Screaming Chaos

By Primary Hollow

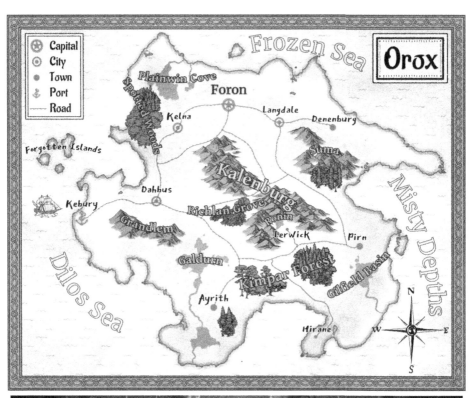

Eliza

"Careful! Don't drop her!" Eliza exclaimed.

Huffing and puffing, Daniel laid Keri's limp body on a patch of crusty grass, then wobbled slightly before leaning on the side of the hill and muttering: "I don't know how much further I can carry her."

Eliza rubbed her nose anxiously before raising her head to the blood moon gleaming in the sky, drenching the mountain passageways in its infernal repugnance.

Suddenly, a horrific scream enveloped everything, sending shivers down Eliza's spine. This was the third time they heard it in the past couple of hours as they wandered the Kalenburg Mountains, trying to find the way out after defeating Fenrir – the last of the three Ancients.

"I thought this was supposed to be over," Daniel said, panting.

"Maybe we were too late," Eliza uttered. "Or maybe Keri was wrong in her conjecture that killing the beast would stop things from escalating."

"What should we do now?"

Eliza lowered her eyes, thinking. Her body, covered with the dirty gown, was shivering from the cold draft blowing through the narrow pathways. She tried desperately to sort out everything that had happened, but her thoughts were jumbled. To make matters worse, there was a faint grumble rising from the darkness of her mind, and she feared that it might be the voice of Dagon, awakened by the howl of the beast, intending to haunt her until she would once more succumb to its will.

Daniel wobbled and gagged several times. Eliza glanced at the large gash gaping on top of his head, angst continuing to build within because of the futility of their situation. "Are you going to be okay?" she asked.

"How the hell would I know?" Daniel grumbled, then gagged again.

Eliza pressed her lips tightly, then stepped toward Keri and knelt beside her, looking at her friend's pale visage, tightly shut eyes, and the gory stump in a place where her right arm used to be before it was bitten off by the Great Wolf. The blood was seeping slowly through the rags they used to cover the wound, and while Keri's chest was still moving, Eliza feared that, without the proper care, her friend wouldn't last much longer.

She extended her hand and gently stroked Keri's disheveled, dirty hair, feeling tears welling in her eyes and her heart fluttering from anguish. "Don't leave me, please," Eliza whispered. "Not now." She lingered for a bit longer, then stood up and glanced at the crimson skies before shifting her gaze back to Daniel. "We need to keep moving."

"Are you sure that we're going the right way?"

"Yes," she lied, giving the man a firm nod. "Come, we need to get out of here as soon as possible."

While Eliza was always known for her exceptional memory, after everything that had happened, she feared that they might've taken a wrong turn or two in their effort to return to Lerwick village. It didn't help that, drenched in the ghastly illumination, the mountains looked completely different than when they first arrived. Still, she didn't want to alert Daniel to the possibility of their wander being aimless to not exacerbate the dread she saw gleaming in the man's eyes.

After resting for a bit longer, Daniel lifted Keri from the ground, cradling her in his arms, and they continued walking forward. Their feet were making eerie squishing sounds on the damp soil, and there were puddles everywhere that now looked like splatters of blood.

The scream came again, piercing the eerie silence of the mountains, making Eliza flinch. She looked over her shoulder at Daniel walking behind her, then was about to resume her amble when a massive lanky creature emerged from the passageway ahead. It had a round head, three yellow eyes, a long horn protruding from the middle of its face, and a giant maw filled with jagged teeth. The demon fixed its leer on the three of them, then opened its mouth, releasing a creepy cackle before commencing its shuffling advance, each step echoing with ominous thuds.

Eliza was the first to act. She raised her magnum and fired three times in rapid succession, all bullets piercing the monster's massive frame. Daniel soon joined her after laying Keri on the ground and grabbing the rifle from his back. Together, they sank at least a dozen shots into the beast's flesh, staggering the creature and drawing the blood that splattered on the ground. But unfortunately, it was not enough to take down the beast since after only a few seconds, the monster recovered and, after grumbling hoarsely, resumed shambling toward them.

"Do you have any more magnum bullets?" Eliza asked, starting to back away.

Daniel shook his head, swung the rifle over his shoulder, then grabbed Keri from the ground. "Perhaps we shouldn't have left the grenade launcher in the valley," he uttered.

Suddenly, the beast released a mad cackle, tilting its head upward before leaning forward and launching into a ferocious charge. Eliza gasped, then fired her last shot, turned, and started running.

They fled through the zigzagging pathways with the monster bellowing and cackling behind them. Eliza could hear Daniel's huffs and puffs, which were quickly becoming heavier. As the massive footsteps approached, she looked over her shoulder to see the creature just a few yards away. After catching her gaze, the beast lunged forward, trying to

4

gore her with its horn, but she dodged just in time. The monster rushed past her, soon catching up to Daniel, and Eliza saw the man stumbling and dropping to the ground, Keri's body slipping from his arms and rolling for a few feet.

The demon stepped toward them and extended its arms, intending to grab both with its grisly claws. Eliza screamed and rushed forward before wrapping her arms around the monster's leg and sinking her few remaining teeth into its flesh, hoping that Keri's power somehow rubbed onto her. But unfortunately, her eyes didn't light up, and her desperate act only served to get the beast's attention as it turned toward her, grinning creepily while gnashing its teeth.

"Take Keri and run!" Eliza screamed. "She's our only hope!"

Suddenly, following a thunderous blast, the monster's head exploded. Eliza felt the heat on her face as she was flung into the air, her back slamming into the sharp rocks. She heard the beast gargle hoarsely. Then, its body was engulfed by a barrage of explosions that brought the creature to the ground, where it twitched several times before finally going limp, its blood and mutilated insides leaking onto the damp soil.

Through her dimming vision, Eliza saw a group of men dressed in military attire stepping into the passageway. One stopped to examine the monster's limp carcass while the others, with guns drawn, approached Eliza, Daniel, and Keri.

"Hey, these ones are still alive!" she heard someone shout, then tried to push off the ground, only to succumb to exhaustion as everything faded into a humming dark.

Christa

Christa got awoken about four hours ago by the first of many ghastly screams. She lay in bed, unsure whether it was just a lingering fragment of one of the nightmares that plagued her since their harrowing escape from Pentara island. But then, she heard the sounds of gunshots accompanied by screams of Daniel's men and crazy demonic cackles that sent shivers down her spine.

Christa did not dare to leave her room, which she shared with Nina, the girl Keri rescued from the Forgotten Islands. Instead, she grabbed the child, who still hadn't spoken since her arrival, and huddled in the corner, peering frightfully at the door.

The memories arose of the hellish hours she spent locked in the guard barracks while being taunted by Daniel's demonic form. Her mind quivered every time the horrible scream came back, and she found herself teetering on the edge of lunacy as she listened to shooting, yelling, and demonic cackling.

Christa whimpered, then pulled Nina closer, looking into the girl's big blue eyes while stroking her curly hair. "We just need to lay low, okay, Nina? Sooner or later, someone will come and save us. We're safe here, and nothing bad will happen as long as we stay quiet."

Nina looked vacantly into Christa's eyes before opening her mouth and releasing a creepy click that sent shivers down the woman's spine. Then, following a tearful yelp, the girl dropped to the ground and started convulsing with foam coming from her mouth and her eyes rolling to the back of her head.

Christa gasped, then grabbed Nina's trembling shoulders, trying to subdue her. The fit lasted for about half a minute before the foam from the girl's mouth gave way to some rancid black sludge that dripped on the floor, forming a disgusting puddle.

Nina lay still for a bit, her eyes tightly shut. Then suddenly, she leaped from the ground, sinking her nails into Christa's cheeks, looking at her with eyes full of ravenous rage before uttering hoarsely: "The void weeps." After these words, the girl grew limp and collapsed to the ground.

Christa stayed still for some time, her heart pounding, feeling blood slowly seeping from several cuts on her face. Then, she leaned toward the girl, extending her trembling hand. "Nina?" she muttered fearfully.

Suddenly, someone knocked on the door, making Christa jump. Seconds later, she heard a familiar male voice that belonged to Darren, one of Daniel's bodyguards: "Christa, are you in there? We need to get out of here!"

"Darren?" Christa uttered, suddenly remembering the prison again and how Daniel tried to trick her into leaving her room. She looked with wide eyes at the door handle moving and felt her teeth beginning to chatter as she sat frozen, afraid to even breathe.

"The palace will soon be overrun!" Darren exclaimed. "We need to leave while we still can!"

"No!" Christa whimpered. "Go away! You're just trying to trick me!"

"Christa, they are coming! We tried to hold them off, but there are just too many of those things. Dozens have died while the others have fled. Daniel told me to look after you two, so please, open the door before it's too late!"

She shifted her eyes to Nina, lying unconscious on the floor.

Can I really risk it? What if it's like before, and the demon is trying to lure me out? On the other hand, if Daniel's men had indeed fallen, this might be our only opportunity to escape. I can't just sit and wait with whatever is happening to Nina. So, I should—

"Christa, please! I can't wait any longer!"

Pressing her lips tightly, she grabbed Nina from the floor and rushed to the door before opening it to see Darren's wide eyes peering from his ashen face. "Thank god," the man uttered, then motioned for her to follow. "Come. Quick."

They ran across the corridor, soaked in crimson light falling through the expansive windows. Christa could still hear some scarce shouts, but they were mostly overshadowed by the demonic cackles and bellows that made her heart quiver painfully in her chest.

Shortly, they reached the stairs descending to the wide hall on the first floor. They managed to get about halfway down when the door leading outside burst open, and through it emerged a gargantuan beast with elephant feet and massive arms, protruding awkwardly from its narrow shoulders and outstretching to just inches above the ground. Sticking out of that enormous frame was a disproportionately tiny head with a pair of beady eyes and no other facial features. The demon was accompanied by two hairy wolfmen and another creature with three wrinkled heads, each with a single bloodshot eye protruding from a bulky frame supported by very long lanky legs.

The beasts looked around the hall before locking their eyes on Darren, Christa, and Nina. Then, following a cacophony of ghoulish war cries, they launched into a ferocious charge.

"Back!" Darren yelled, then turned and began ascending the staircase.

Christa followed him. Soon, they rushed back into the corridor and started running toward the second staircase leading to the backdoor. Christa could hear the approaching excited barks of the wolfmen accompanied by the bellowing of the giant abomination a bit further away.

Suddenly, she felt sharp nails sinking into her flesh, and she shrieked before dodging aside. The two wolfmen ran past her before leaping on Darren, who turned just in time to evade their deathly embrace. He then grabbed the pistol from his pocket and opened fire, hitting one of the wolfmen in the head and splattering its brains before staggering the second one with three shots to its chest.

"Let's go, quick!" Darren screamed.

Christa glanced at the other side of the corridor to see that the three-headed creature had made its way upstairs and was now charging forward while screeching and flailing numerous limbs protruding from its torso. She gasped, then ran past the two wolfmen, slowly rising to their feet despite multiple bleeding bullet holes in their flesh.

She continued rushing, pressing unconscious Nina to her chest, following Darren's figure running before her. Soon, they reached the back of the palace and descended a steep staircase to get to an expansive hall illuminated by large chandeliers with a statue of a man holding a rifle standing in the middle. They ran across, then continued through a narrow corridor before finally reaching the back door, where they paused.

"What if outside is teeming with those things?" Christa asked fearfully.

"It probably is," Darren uttered, putting his ear to the door. He listened briefly, then turned back, looking at Christa intently. "Once we're outside, stick to me as close as possible. We'll run to my jeep in the parking lot and take off."

After Christa nodded, Darren took a deep breath, opened the door, and leaped outside. As they ran, Christa saw guard corpses lying in the meadow with wolfmen and three-headed creatures feasting on their flesh. There were also several downed beasts with their heads splattered or guts spilled, but despite their severe injuries, none seemed fully out of it, still twitching or crawling, trying to get back to their feet.

Somehow, they managed to reach the parking lot unnoticed. There was only a single jeep and two sedans remaining, one of them mangled by some otherworldly force with a corpse of a large man hanging through the broken window. Without stopping, they ran to the jeep that Darren unlocked with a key he pulled from his pocket. Then, he jumped behind the wheel while Christa, with Nina in her hands, hopped in the passenger's seat.

Just as Darren shoved the key in the ignition, there was a loud rumble, and Christa turned her head to see the gargantuan abomination bursting through one of the palace windows before starting to rush straight at them, the ground shaking from its massive stomps.

"We need to go!" she screamed.

Darren pressed on the gas, and the jeep took off with its tires screeching, quickly gaining speed and leaving the monster behind as it bellowed angrily, still chasing after them.

They drove across the crusty meadow and through the palace gates that were now torn off their hinges with more corpses of the guards lying beside the road in pools of their own blood, some still clutching their weapons. Screams and demonic cackles were coming from the city, and Christa saw black smoke rising from the main square.

They took the back road leading to the outskirts, avoiding the car wrecks and more corpses lying on the streets. Soon, they reached the main northern road leading to Kelna and Foron. They saw several cars in the distance, also moving in the same direction. At one point, they were passed by a roadster driven by a man with disheveled brown hair and bloodshot eyes. Beside him sat a woman with a slashed-open bleeding face, wailing hysterically.

Seeing the other survivors made Christa feel slightly better, but her relief was short-lived and was soon replaced by the onset of growing dread as everything was engulfed by another monstrous scream. She turned her head, peering through the window at the massive shadowy figures moving on the horizon, some standing as high as fifty feet tall.

"Better keep your eyes on the road," Darren uttered, clutching the wheel with both hands. "We need to preserve whatever sanity we have left if we want to live through this ordeal."

Faye

Faye was wandering through the murky shadows, trying to find the voice that had guided her for the past few days. The voice that told her all the secrets of the universe and removed all her worry, anguish, and pain. With it gone, all the memories of her past life were slowly creeping in of all the misdeeds she had committed. And it was all just too much to take.

"I'm not a bad person," Faye whimpered, grabbing her head with both hands. "I don't deserve this. I was just trying to get by the best way I could."

"Were you? Really?"

Faye shuddered and turned to see the woman with long blonde hair standing behind her, with the gleam from her sky-blue eye piercing the surrounding fog. The woman smiled broadly, then stepped closer before continuing: "Is this why you shot that poor woman, Faye? Is this why you left her to die in the dirty alleyway? Because you were just trying to get by?"

Faye shook her head while backing away. "I didn't shoot anyone. It was a mistake. It's… It's all your fault!" She suddenly felt rage rising within. "You took everything away from me!"

Faye shrieked and lunged forward, intending to grab the woman by the neck, but as she got closer, the woman's figure faded into the mist, leaving behind only a mocking cackle that was soon also scattered by the cold gust of wind.

Faye stopped and stood still for a while, peering vacantly before her while mumbling, "I don't deserve this," under her breath. Then suddenly, something shifted, and she realized she was standing in the mountain passageway with her bare feet sinking into the wet mud. Then, she felt pain and lowered her gaze to see a large scar on her left forearm surrounded by tiny blisters.

Faye winced, clenching her teeth, then looked around to see a mangled corpse of a man lying on the ground with bones jutting out of his back, all twisted, seemingly from taking a long fall. She gasped, then took a step back before tilting her head to the blood moon gleaming in the sky. She lingered for a bit longer, peering at the ghastly image, noticing shapes on the glowing surface that formed an uncannily twisted monstrous face.

Faye lowered her eyes, feeling her body tremble, then hugged her shoulders and started quickly walking forward, looking around, trying to remember how she ended up in this place. She vaguely recalled getting stuck in the mud by Kalenburg Pass and running with Andre through the mountains from the beastly men that ambushed them and took their belongings. Then, a grisly image of a wolf arose from the darkness of her mind, and she saw her friend's lifeless body hanging between its massive fangs.

Faye whimpered and glanced at the jagged mountain peaks. She then tried to delve deeper into her memories, despite her growing dread. However, whatever happened next was covered in a thick mist, which she could not disperse no matter how hard she tried.

Her bare feet were aching, and the scar on her forearm throbbed painfully, exacerbating her anguished state. Faye whimpered, then leaned on the side of the hill, feeling panic setting in, shortening her breaths and making her heart pound in her chest while the darkest thoughts rose in her quivering mind.

Am I even alive? Is this hell? Perhaps our car got flipped when we swerved off the road, and all that happened next were just posthumous visions of the damned?

Faye whimpered again and was about to drop down, curl into a ball, and try to cry away her sorrows. But then, she noticed something lying on the ground about thirty yards away. At first, she thought it was another corpse, but after getting closer, she realized it was actually a large backpack. The one they took from the woman in Kebury before leaving her to die. Slowly, Faye approached, then crouched down and unzipped it to see two obsidian swords, a shotgun, two boxes of ammo, and a pouch filled with dark-purple powder. She frowned, her anguish now giving way to confusion.

Why would someone drop this bag in the middle of the road? Was whoever took it also chased by the wolf?

Faye hesitated, then grabbed the shotgun, zipped the backpack, and slung it over her shoulder. She checked the gun to see four rounds left before resuming her amble. With her hands gripping the weapon, she felt a bit better – less exposed and vulnerable – and a slight hope glistened at the back of her mind, accompanied by the thought that perhaps not everything was lost yet.

If I could somehow get out of the mountains, maybe I could figure out what in the devil's name is going on. If I managed to reach Langdale, I could sell the swords and put this entire ordeal behind me.

Suddenly, Faye heard a muffled whimper coming from somewhere nearby. She froze, then pressed her back to the side of the hill, listening while holding a firm grasp on her gun. The sound was slowly approaching from where the road was taking a sharp turn. Faye pressed her lips tightly, then pointed the barrel in that direction, put her finger on the trigger, and started to wait.

From behind the corner emerged two women dressed in ragged clothes. One was tall with long curly hair, while the other was a bit shorter with plaited brown hair, and she was the one sobbing and sniffling as they stepped into the open. They were about to walk past when the taller woman noticed Faye and froze before grabbing her companion's arm.

For a while, the three stood in silence, Faye's finger on the trigger trembling slightly and her heart pounding in her chest. Then suddenly, everything was enveloped by a horrific scream that made Faye flinch. Her finger pressed the trigger, releasing the flaming pellets that hit the ground just inches from the women's feet. They gasped and stepped back while the taller one put her arms up. "Wait! Don't shoot!"

"What the hell was that?!" Faye exclaimed, looking around fearfully.

"It has been going on for hours. Is this really the first time you heard it?"

Faye frowned, then stepped forward, her gun still raised. "Do you have any weapons on you?"

"No," the tall woman responded. "Please don't shoot again. They are drawn by the sound."

"They?" A shiver ran down Faye's spine, and she looked around again.

"Could you please lower the gun, so we could explain?"

Faye hesitated a bit longer, then finally lowered the barrel and approached the women, stopping several steps away. "Well, speak," she commanded. "What the hell is going on here?"

Kyron

The expansive hall was illuminated by the soothing light of numerous chic chandeliers hanging from a thirty-foot-high ceiling. In the back, on the gilded, diamond-encrusted throne, sat a man with thick eyebrows and penetrating brown eyes, peering before him from the pale visage framed by medium-length dark-as-night hair. He wore a white jacket with golden buttons, matching pants, and sizable leather shoes. In his hand, he held a silver chalice filled with red wine that he was slowly sipping while watching the massive door on the other end of the hall.

The man's name was Kyron, and he was the sole ruler of Orox ever since he led the continental forces to victory against the rebel army over forty years ago. Since then, he firmly held the power in his hands, eliminating anyone who dared to oppose him. And although the long years had furrowed his face with wrinkles, his spirit was still unyielding and just as lustful for power as when he was just an up-and-coming general. For decades, he managed to uphold peace through fear and respect, and the continent was beginning to flourish, slowly overtaking Talos in its affluence, which was still plagued by inner struggle.

For the longest time, it seemed that no one could challenge Kyron's authority. But everything changed in an instant with a horrendous bellow coming from the west, followed by the appearance of the blood moon that gave rise to misshapen monsters that quickly spread across the land. And while such events sent most of the continent's population into panic, the feeling rising in Kyron's heart was not dread but boundless rage caused by the realization that some force still existed in this world that dared to challenge his sovereignty.

The man took a big gulp of wine, then started tapping on the arm of his throne with his bony finger while peering at the entrance door in an unblinking stare that was not broken even by another ghoulish scream that momentarily enveloped the world.

Soon, the door opened, and a short man with blonde hair wearing a slick military uniform stepped through. His name was Nelson Daley, and he was the Major of the Intercontinental Military Force. He was accompanied by two men wearing dark-blue suits who were a part of Kyron's personal bodyguard crew of over a hundred highly-trained military men.

Daley approached Kyron, stopping about ten yards before the throne, and gave the man a low bow.

"Cut the pleasantries," Kyron grumbled while motioning with his hand. "Tell me what's going on out there."

"The cannons on the inner walls are making quick work of any creatures that try to get close," Daley said. "But unfortunately, the outer city and the slums had been overrun, and the civilian casualties are mounting quickly."

"Why weren't they evacuated behind the walls?"

"The field officers are trying to save whoever they can, but it's pretty hectic out there, and many are devoured by demons even before reaching the gates."

"The beasts must be pushed back," Kyron said firmly. "It's imperative that we give survivors an opportunity to retreat."

"Sir, I don't know how feasible—"

"Just do it," Kyron cut him off. "I will not argue with you, Major. Now tell me about the other cities. Is there any news?"

Daley pressed his lips tightly, then shook his head. "Most communication channels are down. We got a telegram from Denenburg asking for support in the fight against a swarm of flying creatures that descended from the Suma Mountains, but that's it. We also couldn't get in contact with Talos."

"Do you think they could be behind it?"

Daley shook his head again. "Highly doubtful, considering it all started with the attack on Atheta and Pentara. My guess is that we're dealing with intercontinental biological terrorism."

"Biological terrorism?" Kyron frowned. "Is this really the best you could come up with?"

Daley didn't answer, just lowered his eyes to the floor. Kyron sighed, then stood up from the throne. "It seems I'll have to go to the front lines myself if I want to get some answers," he uttered, then motioned with his hand. "Go now. Assemble the troops and push those freaks out of the city. We can decide what to do next after all the surviving citizens are safe."

Daley gave Kyron another bow, then turned on his heel and quickly left the hall. After he left, one of the bodyguards, a tall, burly man, stepped forward and spoke hoarsely: "We have news from the Kalenburg squad."

Kyron raised his eyebrows. "Oh? Did they find something?"

"They found three people wandering the mountains. Two women from Talos, one of whom, from the badge we found on her body, we identified as Atheta's police officer. She was critically injured, so we placed her in the palace's infirmary unit. The last person the crew captured was nonother than Daniel Warner, who, as you know, recently escaped the Pentara's prison. We placed both him and the other woman in the lock-up."

Kyron widened his eyes, then rose from his throne. "Take me to him," he commanded, then, together with his two bodyguards, left the royal hall.

They crossed several wide corridors, their walls decorated with large paintings depicting grisly war scenes, many of them including Kyron himself, leading his troops to battle or standing on the pile of enemy corpses. Shortly, they reached a set of steps that they took to the bottom floor of the Royal Mansion, then crossed a narrow passageway and, through the large arched oak door, stepped into a wide area with twenty holding cells.

The lock-up was illuminated by the dim light of several lanterns hanging from the stone ceiling. All the cages were empty except for the two in the back, holding a frail woman on the right and Daniel Warner on the left.

Kyron had known the man for a long time – ever since Daniel started running his first crew in Dahbus. From the early days, Kyron recognized his great ambition, and on more than one occasion, he chose to step in and help the man to deal with his quarrels against the competing gangs. Through Daniel, Kyron hoped to one day control the entire criminal enterprise. However, as Daniel's authority grew, he more and more often started undermining Kyron's direct orders. Furthermore, rumors were going around about him trying to convince some of the oligarchs to join an assassination plot that would end Kyron's reign. Thus, he decided to act first and set Daniel up to be captured on his trip to Talos and sent to Pentara. Kyron even went a step further and paid off the prison's higher-ups to ensure that the man would not get out before the end of his sentence. In the meantime, he focused his energy on eliminating the oligarchs that proved to be prone to corruption, further cementing his absolute rulership.

A week ago, Kyron got informed that Daniel somehow managed to escape the prison during an alleged terrorist attack and was on his way back to Dahbus, intending to reclaim one of his palaces. Kyron felt absolutely outraged that, despite all his efforts, the man who dared to defy him was walking free again. In different circumstances, seeing Daniel in the lock-up like this – helpless and covered in mud – would have given Kyron a great deal of pleasure. However, considering the severity of the current situation, the only emotion he felt while observing Daniel's sorry state was rage.

"Stand up!" Kyron bellowed, looking at Daniel lying limply on the rough floor.

The man flinched, then pushed off with trembling hands and looked at the ruler of Orox drowsily.

"How dare you sleep at a time like this!" Kyron hollered.

"I think he has a concussion," the bodyguard mumbled.

The ruler of Orox glanced at him, then squinted his eyes, noticing a large gash on top of Daniel's head and a string of drool seeping from the corner of his mouth. Kyron sighed, stepped forward, and banged on the bars, making Daniel flinch again. "Come on, snap out of it. We don't have time for this."

"Kyron?" Daniel uttered.

"Yes, yes. Now speak – what the hell is going on?"

"I-I don't know where to begin."

Kyron clenched his teeth, then turned to the guard. "Unlock it," he commanded.

After the man did as he was told, Kyron took a deep breath, entered the cell, grabbed Daniel by the neck, and slammed him to the wall.

"Hey, don't do that!" the woman from the other cell yelled.

"You shut your mouth!" Kyron bellowed, giving her an angry glare, then turned his attention back to Daniel, who was now gasping for breath and squirming, trying to escape his mighty grip. "Talk, or I'll make you talk!"

Kyron stepped away, releasing Daniel, which made the man slump to the ground. He gagged several times, then looked up. "This is the end of the world," Daniel said hoarsely. "We tried to prevent it, but we failed. The monster will rise from the sea and devour everything that is living."

"Stop speaking nonsense," Kyron grumbled. "I know that you're somehow involved in this. How else could you survive that slaughter in Pentara? Tell me who's behind this and where is your base of operation."

"There is no base of operation," Daniel uttered while getting to his feet. "This is not some political ploy. What is happening is much bigger than any of us."

Kyron raised his fist and punched Daniel in the stomach. The man gasped and fell back to the ground. Meanwhile, Kyron turned and left the cell. "Take him upstairs," he commanded.

"Stop it! He's telling the truth!" the frail woman yelled from her cell.

"Didn't I tell you to shut up?" Kyron shouted, stepping toward her. "You'll have your chance to talk after I'm done with him."

He peered into her willful gray eyes briefly, then turned and exited the room.

Keri

The universe was engulfed by crimson shadows with ghastly howls and demonic cackles echoing throughout the cosmos. Keri was floating in the vast unknown, drifting in and out of existence. Sometimes, she would forget everything about who she was and soar through the empty space, slowly fading into the hollow. But then, she would hear the clanging of chains and see a faint flicker of white light which would bring back the painful memories of her struggles.

Her journey lasted for eternity as she was just a flickering spec soaring through the boundless universe. Then, with another persistent clang, something shifted, restoring her physical shape.

Keri found herself standing amidst a sandy plain, void of any vegetation. She peered vacantly into the distance until she noticed a temple looming on the gray horizon. It was massive, with at least a fifty-foot-high staircase leading to a set of giant Gothic columns framing a rectangular entrance.

Keri lingered briefly, swinging back and forth, part of her still drifting through the boundless space. Then suddenly, everything that had happened came rushing in, and she lowered her eyes to her right arm, expecting to see a gory stump. However, her limb was still there – attached to her shoulder and void of injuries, with the green marking gleaming brightly on her palm.

Keri gazed at the soothing light, feeling the warming sensation spread throughout her shivering flesh. Then, she shifted her gaze to the temple again and started walking forward, each step more firm and decisive than the previous one.

I don't know what this is, but while my spirit is still alive, I'll do everything to find my way back and free the two continents from corruption. I'll do everything to prevent the Maw of the Hollow from devouring my world.

After ascending a few dozen steps, she noticed something glinting in the distance, and when she got closer, she realized that it was a massive greatsword with a silver diamond-encrusted handle lying in the sand. Keri paused, looking at the lump of iron glinting eerily in the dim gray light. Then, she remembered that this was the same weapon she had seen on one of the pedestals in the Castle of Wyrm.

Unsure of what she was doing, Keri stepped forward, leaned over, and grabbed its handle with her right hand. She hesitated, telling herself that surely no mere human could ever wield something like this. Then, she lifted the sword off the ground with surprising ease and raised it into the air.

She felt ancestral energy seeping through where her skin touched the handle, momentarily filling her mind with shadowy whispers. And while Keri couldn't understand what they were saying, she felt the great hatred rising, directed at the corruption and the eldritch beasts, fueling her determination to continue fighting the demons of the void.

She walked quickly toward the temple with the blade resting on her shoulder. Despite its massive frame, the weapon felt almost weightless, and its silver handle felt surprisingly comfortable in her hand. Keri even found excitement building within, awaiting the opportunity to test the sword in battle.

After walking for about a mile, she noticed something moving in the sand. Keri paused, peering warily into the distance, then resumed her amble. Soon, her eyes widened as she beheld hundreds of black eels slithering toward the temple. Then suddenly, from a distance, came a thunderous roar that sent ripples throughout time and space. With it, the bodies of the eels began to twitch and change, growing limbs and turning into the Spawns of the Leviathan that Keri had encountered several times before. They pushed off the ground with their four-fingered claws and started shambling forward, their creepy clicks and grumbles quickly enveloping everything around.

Keri gripped the sword with both hands and looked around nervously, but the beasts didn't seem to notice or care about her presence as they continued ambling forward, their bulging eyes fixed on the distant temple. She hesitated, then resumed moving forward, soon entering the crowd of slimy creatures and walking carefully past them while keeping a firm grip on the sword handle.

After maneuvering through the beastly crowd, Keri overtook them and continued heading toward the temple, now only a mile away. Shortly, the gray skies grew darker, and the dread started creeping back into her mind, slowly overshadowing her initial excitement and determination.

When she finally reached the steep steps, she paused, looking at the obsidian structure before her, with its every inch emanating boundless cosmic malice and hatred as old as the universe itself. Keri looked behind her at the approaching swarm, then lifted her eyes to the darkening skies before taking a deep breath and starting to climb.

It took her a lot longer to reach the top than she initially anticipated, and when she ascended the last step, Keri was out of breath. The sword, which seemed weightless at first, was now pressing painfully into her shoulder, and the dark thoughts began to emerge, giving rise to festering doubt and exacerbating the growing dread.

What if the world is already lost? What if all I see are just echoes reverberating in the boundless universe as my spirit is fading, desperately trying to cling to life through these senseless visions?

Keri lingered, peering at the abyssal darkness looming beyond the massive entrance. Then, she gritted her teeth and stepped inside, deciding that even if the world was lost, there was no point in delaying the inevitable.

If nothingness is what awaits me on the other side, then so be it.

Keri ambled through the dark for some time, shrouded by complete silence that muffled even her footsteps. Then finally, she noticed a faint glimmer in the distance, and soon, she stepped onto the sandy shore outstretching toward the dark waters with a massive obsidian obelisk protruding from the rippling surface.

Wrapped around it was the Leviathan, peering at Keri with its hatred-filled dark eyes. The monster opened its maw, exposing massive grisly fangs, and released a horrible roar, challenging her to another confrontation. With this thunderous bellow, the gray skies turned black, the waves in the sea began to rise, and she heard the distant rumbling of thunder.

With her heart pounding, Keri looked around to see a tiny blue boat standing on the shore with the name "Betsy" written on its side. She hesitated a bit longer, then, following another roar, started quickly walking forward while the rumbling of thunder was getting closer, accompanied by bright flashes of lightning piercing the spectral twilight.

After reaching the boat, she placed the greatsword on the deck and pushed "Betsy" into the water. Then, she hopped inside, grabbed the paddle, and began to row with the Leviathan still eyeing her from a distance.

The storm was approaching, and she could already see the lightning striking the water. There were also whirlpools forming around the obelisk as the waves rose higher and higher, smashing heavily into the hull.

Keri was about fifty yards away from the massive structure when Leviathan released another roar, making lightning bolts come crashing down from the sky, some just yards from Keri's boat. Then, the beast descended from the obelisk and slithered into the rippling waters, its massive figure disappearing into the dark depth.

Keri put down the paddle and grabbed the greatsword. Then, biting her lower lip, her eyes gleaming with bright emerald light, she stood up, peering at the waves, waiting with bated breath for the inevitable attack.

Suddenly, following a loud crack, her boat parted into two, and the massive head of the Leviathan appeared from below, intending to finish

Keri in a single attack. However, she dodged just quickly enough before raising the sword and bringing it down with otherworldly force, the massive blade cutting deep into the monster's neck, drenching her from head to toe with its blood.

The Leviathan shrieked horribly and dove under the water, quickly descending and dragging Keri along, who was clutching the sword stuck in the beast's flesh. Holding her breath, she tried a few times to yank the weapon out with no success. Then, she leaned closer, grabbed the monster with her free hand, and sank her teeth into its open wound.

Abruptly, the reality shifted, and Keri found herself soaring through space and time again. Before her eyes arose visions of an endless ocean laden with countless obsidian obelisks jutting from its surface, each harboring a creature she knew as the Leviathan. She heard the beasts roaring in unison, their wrath rippling through the vastness of the cosmos. Then came the clanging of chains again, and the vision faded, sending her back to drift amidst the looms of time.

Christa

Fearing that the city might be overrun, they took the eastern road going by Kalenburg and around Kelna. They saw many flipped cars along the way and more of the tall figures shambling in the quickly thickening mist, soaked by the gleam of the crimson moon. Nina was still unconscious, and Christa kept glancing at her ashen face, fearing that the child could have another seizure.

"Do you really think we'll be safe in the Capital?" Christa asked.

"The inner city is surrounded by thick walls," Darren said, clenching the wheel of the jeep, his eyes fixed on the misty road. "It's pretty much the safest place in the entire world. If Foron fell, it would mean that all the hope for humanity was lost."

Christa pressed her lips tightly, trying to keep her eyes low and away from the distant demonic figures. She hugged Nina tighter, trying to calm her nerves, thinking that she couldn't afford to lose her mind, at least not until the child was safe. Before leaving, Daniel told her that Nina's family had been killed and she had no one else left in the world. Thus, Christa wanted to protect her at all costs.

"We're not so different, you and I, little one," Christa whispered while carefully stroking the girl's hair.

"What was that?" Darren asked.

"Nothing, don't mind me."

Christa sighed, then extended her hand and opened the glove compartment to see several colorful brochures and an open bag of pretzels.

"You can have them if you want," Darren said.

"I was actually looking for a gun."

The man raised his eyebrows. "Oh? Are you sure you would be able to use one?"

Christa frowned. "What's that supposed to mean? Did you forget that I was a police officer?"

Darren gave her a short glance before fixing his eyes on the road again. "I didn't. I'm sorry. There should be an extra one under the back seat."

Christa leaned over and rummaged briefly before finding a small pistol and shoving it into the pocket of her jeans. She then fixed her eyes on the road ahead and the roofs of tall apartment buildings of the Capital, protruding from the rising mist.

As they were getting closer, they heard distant rumbling and thudding.

"The cannon's on the inner wall are firing," Darren said.

"Can we even get into the city while it's under siege?" Christa asked, her voice trembling.

"We'll just have to find out."

Shortly, they saw the smoke rising, and Darren had to slow down to avoid hitting the broken-down cars scattered on and beside the road, some of them splattered with fresh blood.

"This looks bad," Christa whimpered, her hands beginning to shake.

"We can't turn around now. We're almost out of gas. So, getting behind those walls is our only hope."

Suddenly, the ground parted before them, spitting out yellow burning liquid. Then, from the fissure arose a grotesque giant worm with a long fleshy body and large horns protruding from its head, just above the massive round maw full of sharp fangs. The monster screeched horribly, then lunged, slamming into their car and tipping it over. Darren was launched forward, crashing through the windshield, while Christa hit her head on the roof of the rolling jeep before she was flung through the door, torn open by the impact.

Briefly, everything sank into pitch-black, permeated with a nauseating hum. Christa saw herself soaring above the Kradena Port, looking at her family home enveloped by flames with hordes of demons standing below, their heads tilted toward her as they gnashed their sharp fangs. Then, she was abruptly brought back and, through the haze, saw the worm demon towering above her with green mucus dripping from its disgusting mouth.

Christa gasped, then reached into her pocket, pulled out her pistol, and emptied the magazine into the monster's flesh, splattering the ground with its thick blood. The beast screeched, then withdrew slightly before lunging forward again, and Christa just barely rolled out of the way of its deathly bite.

Suddenly, she heard the shots fired and turned to see Darren standing about twenty yards away, his face covered in deep bleeding gashes with bits of glass stuck in his flesh. She also saw Nina on the ground beside the burning jeep that was flipped on its side.

The monster screeched again and turned to Darren. Meanwhile, Christa hopped to her feet and rushed toward Nina while coughing from the surrounding black smoke. She grabbed the girl, then turned to see the man backing away as the monstrosity slithered toward him, leaving a trail of putrid blood and gore along the way.

"Run!" Christa screamed, then took off herself, sprinting through the muddy field toward the city and away from the smoldering fissure.

She heard another distant screech and looked over her shoulder to see Darren running in the distance, chased by two more giant worms, with the injured one slithering not far behind. Christa gasped, then lowered her head and resumed rushing, squinting her eyes and coughing from the smoke, trying desperately to see something through the surrounding murk.

The thudding of the cannons was getting louder, and she also started hearing scarce roars and demonic cackles coming from the city center. Trying to stay away from the battlefield, Christa stepped onto a narrow pathway meandering through the slums. She followed it for a while before retreating behind one of the ramshackle lodges, spooked by a tall demonic figure looming further ahead.

Trembling, she waited, listening to the loud footsteps and hoarse grunts of the beast as it shambled just past her. She smelled the putrid musty odor and saw a glimpse of a giant swollen head towering above the rooftops of the surrounding houses. Thankfully, the demon was walking away from the town, soon disappearing in the crimson mist.

Christa lingered for a bit longer, then was about to step into the open when someone grabbed her by the shoulder. She jumped and quickly turned, barely keeping herself from screaming, to see Darren standing behind her with his eyes wide and face all bruised and bloody. He raised his finger to his lips, then motioned to follow him.

For a while, they traversed the shadowy alleyways, slowly approaching the city center. The cannon blasts were becoming less frequent, giving way to periods of eerie silence. Then, after another monstrous scream that made Christa whimper tearfully, they finally saw the high walls of the inner city.

Darren peeked behind the corner of the alley they were crossing, then looked back at Christa. "Monsters seem to have retreated," he muttered. "The main gates are not far away from here. Come."

The man stepped into the open. Christa sighed, then pressed Nina tighter to her chest and followed him, trying to ignore the burning sensation in her arm muscles. Quickly, zigzagging between the rubble and passing a few collapsed houses, they reached the main street lined with tall lampposts, most of them bent or torn from their bases. Christa saw wrecked cars everywhere, some with the corpses of the drivers still inside. More dead bodies lay in the street, torn apart, mangled, or missing limbs. Meanwhile, in the distance loomed massive gates with a group of people gathered before them.

"Stay behind me," Darren muttered, then raised his arms and started ambling forward.

Christa took a deep breath and followed him, trying not to step into numerous blood puddles. She noticed that a few mutilated bodies were still twitching, and she quickly averted her gaze, trying her hardest to keep her sanity from breaking, focusing on Nina's slowly-moving chest.

It took them several uneasy minutes to reach the gates. They stopped at the end of the line of about twenty people, most of whom seemed on edge, flinching and whimpering incessantly, some with various injuries and bruises visible through their ripped clothes. Christa saw five soldiers standing in front, thoroughly examining everyone entering the inner city.

After their turn finally came, Darren and Christa were frisked, and their pistols were seized. Then, one of the soldiers asked their names and where they were from, which he wrote down in his notebook. The man then told them they should bring the girl to the hospital on the eastern side of the inner city before finally letting them inside.

As soon as they stepped through, the gates began to close. Christa breathed a sigh of relief and glanced over her shoulder at the mayhem left behind. Then, they started walking to the east, looking at the crowds of people ambling the streets, many staring vacantly into nowhere and mumbling incoherently under their breath. There were also those, who chose to retreat from the horrors in the few still open taverns, and they could hear their drunken cackles as they passed by.

Shortly, the large white building emerged in the distance, and Christa saw a crowd of people gathered beside it, with three soldiers armed with assault rifles standing by the entrance.

"Bring Nina to the hospital," Darren muttered after they stopped at the end of the line.

"Where will you go?" Christa asked, widening her eyes.

"I'll try to find out what the hell is happening. I'll come to the hospital after, okay?"

Christa hesitated before giving the man a short nod. Then, she watched him turn and walk away, his figure soon disappearing behind one of the tall apartment buildings.

Julie

Julie didn't know how much time had passed. It was especially difficult to tell because the blood moon didn't change its position in the sky as if the world had stopped spinning, locked in a nightmare no one could escape. She walked along Sofia through the narrow mountain passageways with the woman who introduced herself as Faye walking behind them, grasping a shotgun in her hands. While she seemed receptive to their story about monsters attacking the village, she was unwilling to trust them completely and chose to keep her distance.

As time passed, Sofia finally stopped whimpering, and the fear in her eyes gave way to the absence Julie remembered seeing when they were locked in the cage by the fish-headed monsters. Julie was on the verge of losing her marbles herself, with Eric's mangled body flashing again and again before her eyes, sometimes accompanied by the vision of Anabel turning into the grotesque beast and stepping through the mirror. When her mind wasn't plagued with horrible imagery, she found herself wondering about the people they saw going to the mountains just before all hell broke loose.

Were they trying to stop this? Did they fail? And if that's the case, what will happen to us? What will happen to the world?

A horrid scream enveloped everything again. Julie looked over her shoulder to see Faye standing with her eyes wide, looking around frantically. "We would feel a lot easier if you pointed that thing to the ground," Julie said, her eyes fixed on the barrel of the shotgun.

Faye pouted her lips before releasing a deep sigh. "I suppose that's fair," she said, lowering the weapon. "I was just looking for the monsters you mentioned or the wolf."

"I'm not sure if the gun would do us any good against those things," Julie said grimly.

"Well, it's better than nothing. Speaking of it…" Faye stopped and took off her backpack.

Julie also stopped, grabbing Sofia by the arm since she seemed content to amble blindly, oblivious to their conversation. Meanwhile, Faye got on one knee, unzipped the bag, and pulled out two swords with black blades and intricate silver handles encrusted with red diamonds. She hesitated briefly, then extended the weapons to Julie. "Here. Not sure how effective these would be, but as I said – better than nothing."

Julie took the swords, looking at them warily. She noticed they had distinct engravings on their handles – one depicting a dragon while the other showcased a barking dog. "These look like decorative antiques. Are you sure that rocks wouldn't be more effective?"

Faye shrugged. "Suit yourselves. I don't have anything else."

Julie hesitated, then shoved the sword with the dog into Sofia's hands. "Hold this."

Sofia nodded, grasping the handle, her eyes still peering blindly before her. Meanwhile, Faye zipped the bag and threw it back on her shoulders.

"Do you have anything else in there?" Julie asked.

Faye shook her head. "There's only a pouch filled with some powder. Probably drugs. But it doesn't seem like the best time to have a party."

Julie smiled faintly, then sighed and resumed her amble. They continued through the damp stony passageway for a while longer until they saw something glinting in the distance. After sharing a silent glance, Julie and Faye hastened their pace. Soon, the tall mountains parted, and they stepped into the expansive field with a forest of tall trees looming a bit further away.

"Richlan Grove," Faye said. "We made it out."

The three stopped, looking around, listening for any sounds, but the only thing they could hear was the wind howling in the mountains behind them.

"Should we take the Pass?" Julie asked.

"I would rather head to Dahbus," Faye said. "I also think that we should stay away from the road, maybe walk close to the treeline so we could retreat to the grove if needed."

"Sounds like a plan."

"What do you think, Sofia?" Faye asked, looking at the woman intently.

Sofia wobbled slightly after hearing her name, then muttered a short "sure" before tilting her head and fixing her eyes on the blood moon.

Faye shifted her gaze back to Julie. "Will she be okay?"

"We'll be fine as long as we can get out of here."

Faye lingered a bit longer. Then, she finally nodded, and they resumed walking forward, positioning themselves between the grove and the main road.

Daniel

Daniel was lying limply on the rough floor of his cell. Most of his body was numb, and there was a persistent ringing in his ears, muffling all the other sounds. After he was taken upstairs, Kyron asked him to tell the truth, and when he did, he was beaten mercilessly by two of Kyron's men. Then, the ruler of Orox asked him the same question, and Daniel repeated his story just to be punished again. His torture lasted for hours until he could no longer speak, at which point he was returned to his cell and dropped unceremoniously on the ground, where he lay gasping, trying not to choke on his own blood.

Eliza tried to speak to him from the other cell, but he couldn't understand her as he drifted in and out of consciousness. When he finally regained some of his senses, through a haze, he saw something vaguely familiar crawling from the shadowy corner of his cell. Daniel gathered whatever mental capacity he still had left, trying to remember what it was. But what arose from the darkness of his mind made his battered body shudder in the utmost terror.

Daniel gasped a few times, then tried to push away from the tiny spec of black mass with dozens of small tendrils slowly crawling toward him. Meanwhile, he heard a demonic whisper in his ear, temporarily silencing the nauseating hum: "Why are you trying to reject me, Daniel? I already told you that your struggle is futile, and your fate is sealed. No matter what happens next, after your link with this world is broken, you will return to my domain as your final resting place. So why do you choose to suffer? Would it not be so much easier to embrace my gift once more and take revenge on those who wronged you?"

"No," Daniel squeezed out, then started coughing, sputtering blood from his mouth.

"Don't you want to feel all-powerful again?" the Corpse Crawler continued. "There were times when you would've done anything for such an opportunity. Or did you already forget your ambition?"

The quivering mass was slowly approaching while Daniel continued whimpering, trying desperately to push away, but his battered flesh refused to listen. Eliza was screaming something from the other cell, but her words still eluded his comprehension as he tried to back away. However, despite his efforts, the *thing* eventually reached him, and he felt its tendrils burrowing into his leg.

The cell abruptly disappeared, and Daniel found himself standing amidst the boundless wasteland of rough crimson rock. As far as his eyes could see, bodies were shambling about, bound by tentacles wrapped around their decaying flesh. All these writhing limbs outstretched from the gargantuan being looming on the horizon.

Daniel heard a horrific cackle that froze the blood in his veins, and he saw numerous feelers soaring toward him. He gasped, then turned around and started running as fast as he could. He stumbled over the sharp rocks, trying to avoid the zombified humans, animals, and beings he had never seen before. They were all wailing and gargling, trying to grab him with their rotting limbs, all controlled by the Corpse Crawler – the ancient malice of the void.

Suddenly, Daniel felt someone grabbing his arm and yanking it firmly, making him tumble. He turned his head to see Wesley, the descendant of hillfolk, and Taylor, his former cellmate, standing over him. Smiling broadly, both men lunged forward and pinned his hands to the ground.

Daniel squirmed desperately, his eyes darting from their uncanny grins to the tentacles soaring through the air. Moments later, they wrapped around his waist and neck, squeezing and pulling while the demon spoke inside his head, mocking his struggle and commanding him to succumb to its will and drift into the screaming dark.

Daniel was about to let go, but at the last moment, as his sanity was slipping into the pit of eternal wailing madness, he remembered Keri; and the emerald gleam he saw in her eyes when she sank her teeth into the demonic flesh. He also recalled the feeling of lightness that followed as he glimpsed for a split second at the vastness of the universe and the dark secrets lurking between the cosmos.

Suddenly, the faces of Thomas and Mark, his two best friends, arose before his eyes.

"You can do it, boss," Thomas said, giving him a little wink.

"Come on, bud," Mark added. "Let's get out of this place."

Daniel reached out his hands toward them, still feeling the tentacle squeezing his neck and hearing the gargles coming from his mouth. But his suffering was now muffled as his spirit flickered between the dimensions. Mark and Thomas grabbed his hands, the coldness from their palms seeping through his skin and pushing away the demonic presence. Then, Daniel heard the Corpse Crawler's angry bellow and saw a flash of white light accompanied by a sharp clanging of chains. Finally, he was brought back to his cell, gasping frantically and spitting blood from his mouth.

With his fading vision, he saw the black mass leaving his flesh and crawling back to the corner from which it came. Seconds later, his mind went blank, and he drifted into the humming void.

Kyron

With a loud rumble, the inner city gates began to open. Kyron looked around the brigade of about a hundred men standing before him armed with rifles, shotguns, grenade launchers, and pistols. There were also four trucks with mounted miniguns, two military ambulances, and a tank, one of the last few left after the war. Major Daley stood beside him with his chest puffed and head tilted, calm and composed despite the horrors they were about to face.

"Can we take back the city and establish the perimeter in a single push?" Kyron asked.

Daley nodded. "Yes, Sir. Although I need to advise you once more to send a few scouting parties first to assess the strength of the enemy forces."

"We don't have time for that, Major. My people are dying. We must take back the city and restore communications with the rest of the continent as soon as possible."

"The problem is that we still have no idea what we're dealing with."

"Well, we're not going to find out by cowering behind the walls," Kyron said firmly.

Daley glanced at him, then nodded before turning his gaze to the destruction outstretching behind the gate. The main street, once bustling, was now laden with car wreckage, rubble, and mutilated corpses of men and beasts, splattered across the pavement.

The Major took a big breath, then spoke in a firm, clear voice: "Move out! Don't hesitate to shoot the enemy, but be on the lookout for the survivors."

Following his command, the brigade started advancing with the tank chugging in front, two trucks with miniguns driving on each side while the infantry trailed close behind. Meanwhile, Kyron and Daley boarded one of the ambulances, which joined the back of the formation.

Kyron sat by the tinted window, looking warily at the collapsed buildings slowly moving past them. He was clenching the gilded handle of his magnum revolver, the same one he used during his military service days. It has been decades since Kyron saw actual combat. Still, he made an effort to retain his physique and keep his skills sharp by frequenting a shooting range and keeping up with the daily rigorous exercise regime. And while he started noticing some signs of physical decline during the past five years, inside, the man still felt just as vigorous as ever, and he wasn't going to allow anyone to take away what he had worked so hard to achieve.

Whether those freaks are mutants born from biological experiments or actual devils that crawled from the pits of hell, I will push them back and reclaim my land, even if it's the last thing I do.

Slowly, they were moving away from the inner city toward the shabby lodges in the slums. There were still no signs of the ghoulish attackers, and while they came upon more wrecked cars and human corpses lying in puddles of their own blood, they failed to find any survivors.

Shortly, they reached the edge of the town and stopped at an intersection with the paved road leading to Kelna and several dirt pathways meandering into the slums. Major Daley grabbed his radio, pressed the button, and spoke: "The front formation, do you see anything? Over."

"The main road to Kelna is covered in thick white mist," one of the soldiers responded. "We noticed some figures shambling in the distance. However, they're too far away to get a clear view and seem unwilling to engage. Over."

Daley pondered briefly, then turned to Kyron: "Should we start establishing the perimeter? The city seems clear."

Kyron nodded. "Yes. Contact the remaining forces, and tell them to start moving out and positioning themselves in the main intersections. Also, send a few small squads to check out the slums. After we confirm that the entire city is secure, we'll start moving toward Kelna."

"Even with all this mist? The soldiers said they saw something. So, the enemy might be preparing an ambush or the second wave of attacks."

"You're not here to question my decisions, Major," Kyron grumbled. "From now on, if I want to hear your opinion, I'll ask for it myself. Understood?"

Daley glanced at Kyron, then nodded while pressing his lips tightly before raising the radio to his mouth again and beginning to bark out orders. Meanwhile, Kyron leaned back in his chair, peering at the crimson twilight seeping through the window. He then tilted his head and looked at the blood moon gleaming in the sky. Somehow, it seemed bigger than before, and the markings on its surface were clearer, reminiscent of a grinning face. Still, even such realization did not cause dread to rise in the man's mind. Although, he once more felt the rage building because of his inability to take a firm grasp on the situation.

"Tell everyone to hurry up," Kyron uttered, his eyes still fixed on the ghastly moon.

Daley nodded, then was about to speak into the radio again when a loud screech came from the device, which sounded like hundreds of demonic voices, shrieking in unison. Seconds later, they heard the beastly scream again. Briefly, it enveloped everything, and Kyron saw a few soldiers cowering in the formation with their hands pressed to their ears.

He was about to bring this act of cowardice to Major's attention when, just seconds after the scream ceased, the ground beneath them quaked, and the street parted in a large explosion that launched many soldiers into the air while drenching others with burning yellow liquid.

Out of the fissure emerged ten giant worms with large horns protruding from their heads. The monsters lunged at the nearest soldiers, biting, gnawing, and ripping them limb from limb. Meanwhile, the others started firing their pistols and shotguns, and Kyron saw a few men falling to the ground, maimed by the bullets of their comrades.

"Back away!" Major screamed into the radio. "Watch the crossfire!" He jumped out of the ambulance, grabbed the rifle from his back, and started shooting at the attacking beasts.

Meanwhile, Kyron sat still, listening to the screams of the injured soldiers and shrieks of the eldritch worms. His heart was pounding, and he felt a slight tremble in his hand that was clutching the revolver. It took him a few seconds to get a hold of himself and leave the car. Once outside, Kyron leaned against the truck and aimed his gun at one of the three remaining worms that were trying to bite at the troops while their flesh was riddled with an avalanche of bullets, splattering blood and goo in all directions.

Kyron was about to shoot when he noticed something moving in the corner of his vision. He quickly turned, peering at the red skies streaked with dark clouds moving toward the city. He paused, then widened his eyes and took a step back, suddenly realizing that these clouds were actually swarms of winged demons soaring toward them.

"Behind us!" Kyron bellowed. "In the sky!"

Although some soldiers continued firing at the mutilated worm corpses, most turned and tilted their heads. Moments later, someone started screaming, and Kyron saw at least two men fleeing the battlefield. Nonetheless, most surviving troops, including the ones manning the miniguns, began blasting at the upcoming horde.

Dozens of leathery bodies fell from above, smashing onto the pavement and rooftops. However, more beasts were coming. Shrieking horribly, they charged the troops, biting and tearing their flesh with sharp claws. Agony-filled screams broke out, and bullets started flying everywhere, downing many in the crossfire. Daley was shouting directions between his rifle shots, but his voice was muffled by the chaos raging around them.

Meanwhile, Kyron was crouching behind the ambulance, downing the attacking demons with precise blasts. He emptied the chambers of his revolver, then started reloading. This was when three demons landed before him, peering at him with purple-gleaming eyes while brandishing their claws and gnashing their fangs.

Bullets slipped out of Kyron's hands. Moments later, the closest beast lunged at him, trying to take a swipe. Fortunately, the man was quick enough to back away before grabbing his secondary handgun holstered to his waist.

He emptied the magazine, downing the attacking beast. However, its place was immediately taken by the two remaining demons, undeterred by the slaying of their kin. They rushed the man, swinging their claws wildly. Kyron tried to dodge again, but this time he was too late, and he felt sharp nails sinking into his chest. He gasped, then dropped to the ground and rolled to the side, trying to escape. However, the demons followed him, grabbing his ankles and yanking him backward before sinking their fangs into his legs.

Kyron bellowed in pain, then grabbed the knife strapped to his thigh and stabbed one of the creatures in the neck, slicing through disgusting growths pulsating on its skin that broke, splattering rancid goo and blood on Kyron's face. At the same time, the head of the second beast exploded in a cloud of gore. The man turned to see Major Daley leaning against the building about ten yards away, aiming his rifle.

Following the second shot, the demon with the bleeding neck was flung backward and dropped to the ground, where it released a gargling shriek before going limp. Daley rushed to Kyron and helped him to get up before yelling: "More of them are coming! We need to get out of here!"

They retreated into the ambulance, avoiding several aerial swipes from the demonic creatures swarming the skies.

"Go!" Daley screamed at the young soldier in the driver's seat. Then, he grabbed his radio and started shouting: "Retreat back to the inner city! Ready the cannons! Order all the surviving civilians to go indoors and barricade the entry points!"

With the tires of the ambulance screeching, they took off. The driver made a sharp turn before stepping on the accelerator. Kyron saw the hands of the young recruit trembling, and he thought that he should probably take over before the boy got them killed. But then, he felt a sharp pain that surged through his body, momentarily shackling him from head to toe as a loud moan escaped his mouth.

"Sir, are you okay?" Daley asked, turning toward him.

"I'll be fine," Kyron uttered through clenched teeth. "These damned things! How come no one saw them coming? We need to—"

Suddenly, following a thunderous bellow, a gargantuan creature leaped from behind one of the tall apartment buildings. The abomination had wrinkly elephant feet and long arms hanging from its narrow shoulders. It slammed into their car with its massive frame, lifting the vehicle into the air. They crashed into the building across the street before rolling a few times.

For a moment, everything went dark, and Kyron felt like he was floating in the shadowy void with tearful screams coming from somewhere very far away. Then, he was brought back to find himself lying upside down, his face pressed to the car's roof. The young soldier was lying a bit further away, his head sticking through the broken windshield and his eyes wide and devoid of life.

"Sir, we need to get out of here!" he heard Daley's voice and felt the Major's hand grabbing his wrist.

Ignoring the many pains throbbing in his battered flesh, Kyron managed to get up and get out through the torn-open doorway on the passenger's side. He raised his gaze to see Daley standing beside him with a large piece of glass stuck in his belly and blood seeping from his cracked lip.

"Sir, we need to—" the Major began to say when they heard the horrific bellow again, and both turned to see the giant abomination charging at them at full speed.

Daley grabbed his pistol and started firing but only got two shots out, hitting the creature's frame but failing to impede its advance. The beast lunged forward and slammed the Major into the wall with one hand while grabbing Kyron with the other and lifting him into the air.

Through a haze, the ruler of Orox peered at the black beady eyes staring at him from a disproportionately small head. Feeling the otherworldly malice radiating from the monster's gaze, the fear finally overtook him, and he started screaming and squirming, trying to escape. But unfortunately, his struggles proved futile, as the beast's grasp was only becoming tighter.

Kyron started gasping, feeling his ribs breaking and fragments of bone puncturing his lungs. He gargled as blood shot from his mouth and nose, and the world started fading into the shadow.

Suddenly, following a loud rumble, the beastly frame exploded. Kyron felt a wave of heat washing over him before his body was flung aside, slamming into the brick wall of the nearby apartment building before dropping heavily onto the pavement. He heard the soldiers screaming and the demons screeching, and he saw the tank approaching from the distance. Then, everything blended into a shrieking jumble of color and shadow permeated by a repugnant crimson gleam, followed by the impenetrable dark that Kyron did not expect to awake from.

Christa

Christa stood beside a hospital bed where Nina lay with her eyes closed, her chest slowly moving up and down. Darren stood beside her, his face covered in bandages. There were about fifty beds in total in the massive hospital ward, all occupied by people with varying degrees of injuries. Some lay limply like Nina, while others were sobbing or outright wailing from pain and mental distress. A single doctor and three nurses were doing their best to attend to everyone's needs, but they all seemed exhausted and on the verge of breaking.

"Did they check her yet?" Darren asked.

"Yes, but the doctor couldn't tell what was wrong. He told me she may be in a shock-induced coma and that we should watch her closely and inform him if her condition worsens."

Darren sighed, looking into Nina's pale face, then peered out the expansive windows of the room at the blood moon gleaming brightly in the sky.

"How about you?" Christa asked. "Did you find what you were looking for?"

Darren stood still for a bit, then looked around before leaning closer to Christa and whispering: "I met with one of my contacts in the Royal Palace. He told me that Daniel and some foreign woman are being held captive in the lockup."

Christa widened her eyes. "Could it be Keri?"

Darren shrugged.

"What about Thomas and Mark?"

Darren shrugged again, then leaned even closer. "I heard they may be torturing them, trying to get the information. Kyron thinks that Daniel is somehow involved in all this mess."

Christa's heart fluttered uncomfortably, and her eyes trembled, remembering how she saw Daniel lying in prison's infirmary after the beating he took from Wesley. "We need to get them out," she mumbled, then shifted her gaze back to Nina. "But… we can't just leave her like this."

"I'll go," Darren muttered. "I got a pistol from the same contact, and he told me to return in a few hours. Kyron is currently leading an operation to free the city from monsters, so we might be able to sneak into the palace unnoticed."

Christa pressed her lips tightly, thinking, then gave Darren a short nod. "Alright."

"We may not see each other before this is over. But you just stay put, okay? Take care of Nina while I—" Darren stopped mid-sentence. His eyes widened, and he took a step back with his mouth hanging open.

"What's wrong?" Christa asked fearfully, then turned to the window to see a swarm of horrific demonic entities soaring at them while flapping their broad, leathery wings.

The ward broke out in a cacophony of horrified screams as more people noticed the approaching infernal horde. Those who could, leaped from their beds and started sprinting toward the exit, while others just watched with their eyes wide, shackled by insurmountable horror.

Christa grabbed Nina and, together with Darren, started running for the exit when the expansive windows of the ward shattered into tiny pieces, and the monster started pouring inside. The people huddle by the single door, trying to squeeze through. Meanwhile, the demons started attacking the helpless patients, biting and ripping them apart.

A particularly grotesque beast, slightly bigger than the others, with long sharp horns protruding from its forehead, cut Christa and Darren off before lunging at them, trying to take a swipe. The man pushed Christa behind him. Then, he grabbed the pistol hidden under his shirt and started shooting, sinking three bullets into the monster's head and bringing the beast down. However, it was immediately replaced by three other demons, forcing Christa, Darren, and one of the nurses into the corner of the room.

Gnashing their grisly fangs, the creatures were approaching. Darren fired a few more times, emptying the magazine, clipping two beasts but failing to take any of them down. Christa's heart was pounding like crazy, her gaze darting from the demons still pouring inside to the people trampling over each other, trying to get out. The casualties were quickly mounting as the beasts were slaughtering everyone indiscriminately.

Two more creatures joined the three demons surrounding them, exacerbating the graveness of their situation. Whimpering, her back pressed against the wall, Christa looked at Nina to see her eyes wide open. While usually blue, they were now gleaming with emerald light that pierced through the ghastly crimson, radiating a soothing warmth.

The girl opened her mouth, and out of it erupted an ear-piercing shriek followed by a massive wave of energy that washed over the ward. The bodies of the closest demons exploded in a disgusting cloud of gore and mucus while the remaining beasts were pushed back through the shattered windows, also taking out a part of the wall.

For a moment, Christa, Darren, and the nurse stood unmoving, trying to grasp what had just happened. Then, their daze was shattered by the rattling of the minigun coming from outside, and they saw the demonic swarm flying away.

Christa lowered her gaze to Nina, who lay limply in her hands with her eyes tightly shut. She then looked at Darren, whose brow was furrowed in confusion. Shortly, they heard the soldiers shouting outside. Darren quickly put the pistol back under his shirt, then glanced at the nurse beside them and muttered: "Not a word about this, understood?" After the woman nodded, he grabbed Christa by the arm, and they quickly exited the ward.

Keri

Keri saw the faces of Police Chief Graham and his wife Layla as they stood beyond the temple, looking at the vastness of the sea, listening to the Leviathan's call. Their skin was rippling, and their limbs were twitching from the desire ingrained in their flesh, urging them to join their master. They lingered for a while, holding each other by the hand before turning to Keri standing behind them. She saw tears in Graham's eyes and noticed his mouth moving, trying to tell her something, but she couldn't discern a single word through the nauseating hum.

Suddenly, an icy cold washed over her, accompanied by piercing demonic cries. Keri opened her eyes to see Christa leaning over her, trying to shield her from the approaching winged beasts. Then, feeling energy pulsating within, Keri opened her mouth and released a thunderous scream that momentarily enveloped everything around. Then, she felt herself rising and soaring through the cosmos again, seeing billions of galaxies emerge and fade back into the void in an endless cosmic waltz.

Following a flash of blinding bright light, Keri felt a solid ground under her feet. She looked around, realizing that she stood in a massive white hall with hundreds of steep staircases leading to hundreds of doors of various shapes and sizes. Unsure of what was happening, Keri took a few steps forward, dragging her massive sword on the floor, trying to decide which door to try first. Then, she heard someone scurrying behind her, and she quickly turned to see Nina clad in a long white dress, standing with a broad smile on her face.

"Hello, Miss Keri," Nina chirped. "The white lady told me you'd be coming."

Keri raised her eyebrows. "The white lady?" She looked around before fixing her eyes on the girl again. "Nina, do you know where we are?"

The girl pressed her tiny finger to her cheek, pouted her lips, and raised her eyes, seemingly thinking deeply. She stood still for a bit before smiling again and giving Keri a shrug. "I'm not sure. But I know the way out. Follow me."

Nina turned on her heel and started walking quickly across the hall. Keri hesitated, then raised the greatsword, placed its blade on her left shoulder, and followed Nina, their footsteps echoing loudly in the surrounding tranquility.

They walked for several minutes before reaching an old wooden staircase, ascending to a small door covered in moss and brown fungi. Nina climbed a few steps, then turned to Keri while pointing at the door with her finger. "Your path leads through there."

Keri stood still, looking at the door, feeling shivers running down her spine and the humming in her ears becoming louder. "What's behind it?" she asked with a slight tremble in her voice.

"Your destiny," Nina whispered, something peculiar glinting in her blue eyes.

"Destiny? What do you mean?"

Nina shrugged. "I don't know, Miss Keri. I've only been told to bring you here."

Keri looked into Nina's eyes for a bit longer, then gripped the handle of her sword more firmly and started ascending the steps. When she was about midway, she heard Nina's voice again: "Miss Keri?"

She turned to see tears glinting in the girl's eyes.

"Thank you for saving me," Nina said, then hopped down the stairs and ran across the hall before disappearing in a flash of bright light.

Keri lingered for a bit longer, trying to determine whether she was in some comatose dream, in some other world, or maybe in a posthumous realm where she was transported after succumbing to her injuries in her fight against Fenrir. Then, after not finding any answers in the shimmering darkness within, she turned and ascended the staircase before extending her arm and pressing her palm to the damp, rotten surface of the door.

Keri pushed lightly, producing a loud creak, and she sensed a faint breeze coming from the other side, carrying a disgusting musty smell. After the door fully opened, she felt a light tug. Then abruptly, the white hall disappeared, giving way to a boggy marsh.

A thick layer of mist covered the ground with loose branches and the tops of tiny shrubs sprouting from underneath. Carefully, Keri started sloshing onward, trying to avoid tripping in the mud. She heard a distant buzzing of mosquitoes and a croaking of frogs, and she deliberated whether she should move toward the sounds. But in the end, she decided to head in the opposite direction toward the dense grove looming about a mile away.

As she was getting closer, the musty smell got more potent, and she saw that all the trees in the grove were dead and rotten, their naked black branches swaying eerily in the wind. Then suddenly, she heard a loud shriek and saw a massive bird rising from the thicket before flying over her head and disappearing in the greenish skies.

Startled, with her heart pounding, Keri lingered, gripping the handle of her sword and looking for any signs of life. After not hearing anything for some time, she resumed trudging toward the dead grove. Soon, she stepped onto the black soil, still muddy but much easier to traverse. Then, she started ambling between the trees, breathing the musty stench so potent that it made her retch a few times.

Keri didn't know how long she walked, but when she stopped, she felt disoriented. She sighed and leaned on the nearby trunk, taking deep breaths, foul fetor of death filling her lungs. Suddenly, she heard something rustling behind her, and she turned to see a ghastly creature by one of the trees about fifty yards away, peering at her with its yellow eyes.

The beast stood about six feet tall, and it had swollen gray lips and a lanky body covered with brown fur. After catching Keri's gaze, it opened its mouth, baring its disgusting yellow teeth, before releasing a sharp shriek that sank deep into her mind, making her temples throb painfully and strengthening the nauseating hum in her ears.

Keri staggered and stepped back, slamming into the trunk, sinking slightly into the rotten wood as if it was a fleshy cadaver of some dead animal. She grabbed her sword, gritting her teeth, looking at the beast as it looked back at her. Then, from the corner of her eye, she saw another similar creature, slightly shorter, peeking from the tree to her right. With her body trembling, Keri looked around to see at least ten creepy fiends leering at her ominously, baring their teeth, their bony hands clutching the trunks they were standing by.

Slowly, Keri started backing away. The first monster shrieked again, making her wince in pain. It then stepped from behind the tree and started shambling toward her. The other beasts soon followed, and as Keri continued backing away, she saw more and more of the grotesque heads popping out, their numbers growing by the moment.

She turned and started walking quickly, looking over her shoulder every few steps. The beasts had also increased their pace, drenching everything in eerie rustling as they dragged their hairy feet through the mud. Suddenly, Keri heard a hoarse bellow coming from the distance. She paused for a second, listening. Then, the sound returned, resembling not the beastly scream but one of a person calling for help.

Keri looked over her shoulder once more before taking off, rushing through the mud and zigzagging between the trees. After a few minutes, the grove parted, and she stepped into a clearing with a giant tree in the middle, at least thirty feet thick and as tall as the sky. Its trunk was covered in yellow moss and disgusting pulsating growths filled with rancid liquid. Its massive roots were sticking out of the ground and moving constantly, making the soil ripple as if it was infested by hundreds of snakes.

Trapped amidst that quivering nightmare was a man with short gray hair. He turned toward Keri, and after their eyes met, she realized that it was Leonard, the last descendant of Wyrms who had fallen in the battle against the witch on Pentara island. He was clutching an obsidian sword with the dragon handle, swinging it wildly, trying to get out, but with every move, he sank deeper into the bubbling mud.

Keri gritted her teeth and rushed forward, cutting through the living roots that were trying to grab her. After reaching Leonard, she started hacking away at his living prison. More roots were sprouting from the soil, and she heard the angry shrieking of the furry creatures shambling into the clearing from all sides.

Finally, Keri managed to set the man free. After she helped him to get up, they rushed through the bubbling clearing, ripping through the ranks of the beasts trying to grab them. With a combined effort, they reached the grove and continued moving while slashing at their creepy assailants.

Shortly, the ghoulish creatures started retreating, leaving behind dozens of slashed-open corpses of their kin. Keri and Leonard stopped, panting and looking around before fixing their eyes on each other.

"So you had fallen too?" Leonard uttered hoarsely.

"I'm not sure," Keri said. "I killed the three ancients, but I don't think it was enough."

The hunter gave her a thorough look, his gaze settling on the greatsword in her hand. "Did you go back to Exter?" he asked.

"I did, but it is not where I got the sword." Keri straightened her back, then pressed her lips tightly, looking at the hunter's wrinkled visage. "Leonard, what happened to you?"

The man sighed and lowered his eyes before uttering: "I lay bleeding in that cursed place until I could bleed no more. Then, the darkness came, and when I woke up, I was trapped beneath that damn tree."

"I shouldn't have left you down there," Keri said. "I should've brought you back home."

Leonard sighed again. "It doesn't matter now. Let's try to find a way out of this place before those fiends return."

They took another minute to catch their breath before starting to amble onward through the dead woods, keeping an eye out for the monsters that may be hiding behind the rotten trunks. Once more, Keri found herself drifting into a deep brooding, wondering about the implications of their meeting.

Am I actually dead? And if I am, what is the purpose of this journey? To free the tortured spirits I left along the way? Or is this my personal hell where I'm cursed to struggle for eternity, reliving different versions of my past?

"I was told that no human could ever wield that sword," Leonard said, awakening Keri from her dark thoughts.

"Then why was it made?" she asked, raising her eyebrows.

Leonard shrugged. "Who knows at this point. My ancestors were a pretentious bunch. Perhaps the greatsword, just like the ghastly paintings and the statues in the castle, was crafted to intimidate. To imply that a Wyrm might've existed who could carry such a thing into battle."

They grew silent again. After several minutes of walking, Keri picked up the croaking of frogs, similar to the one she had heard when she first arrived at this place. She noticed something glinting in the distance, and shortly, they stepped out of the woods into an expansion of boggy landscape dotted with patches of dark, murky water surrounded by reeds and tall grass. In the middle of the marsh lay a massive lake, its surface glinting in the greenish illumination falling from the sky.

Keri noticed several giant frogs drowsing on the shore, each at least four feet tall with their slimy skin riddled with disgusting rashes and twitching growths. She gazed at the monstrous beasts, then turned to a massive structure rising from the mud a bit further away, vaguely reminiscent of a house carved inside a giant mushroom. It was riddled with numerous crevices and protrusions, filled with disgusting blue moss and multicolored fungi. At the bottom was a tiny doorway framed by a twisted, gnarled wood pulsating and writhing as if trying to break free.

"This is it," Leonard muttered, and Keri felt a tremble in his voice.

"What do you mean?" she asked.

Leonard turned toward her, his dark eyes wide and full of terror. "The being that took my life and got a grasp on my spirit. This is where she lives – Heket, the baleful witch of the swamp."

Keri felt shivers running down her spine as she looked at the structure before them, noticing more pulsating sections as if it was all part of a single living thing. She took a deep breath, then started walking forward, gripping her sword with both hands. After taking several steps, she looked over her shoulder to see Leonard still lingering by the tree line.

"Come," Keri said. "Slaying the beast is our only way to get out of here."

"And what comes next?"

"That I do not know. But anything is better than being stuck in this horrible place, wouldn't you agree?"

The man lowered his eyes, thinking deeply. Then finally, he gave her a nod, stepped onto the boggy soil, and they started sloshing toward the witch's house.

"Keep an eye on those frogs," Keri mumbled. "They seem docile now, but I wouldn't be surprised if Heket tried to send them after us."

The building turned out to be much further than it looked at first, as if it was moving away from them as they tried to get close. But eventually, they reached the doorway and, after sharing an uneasy glance, stepped through the quivering frame.

Once inside, they crossed a narrow corridor soaked in blue illumination before reaching a massive chamber with walls made from some fleshy throbbing substance. The air here was stale, permeated with a pungent stench of mold and decay. The only sound they heard was a faint rustling, seemingly coming from the walls themselves, that pulsated slightly like the insides of some giant organism.

In the center of the room stood a throne made from thick roots sticking out of the muddy ground. On top of it sat the witch Heket, clad in a ragged gray robe, her skin covered in disgusting pulsating blisters filled with rancid goo. Her wrinkled head hung low, her eyes framed by the horrifically twisted face were shut, and her chest heaved in a slow rhythm.

"Could it be sleeping?" Leonard whispered.

"I wouldn't count on it," Keri muttered. "More likely, this is some kind of a trap."

Slowly, she raised her sword, stepped inside the chamber, and started ambling forward, trying not to make a sound. Leonard followed behind her, also readying his weapon for the inevitable confrontation. Shortly, they stopped a few yards before the throne. With disgust, Keri looked at the rancid blue drool seeping from the witch's mouth, and she heard a hoarse gargling accompanied by a strange muffled buzzing and clicking.

Biting her lower lip in agitation, Keri looked at Leonard, who gave her a nod. Then, they both lunged forward, sinking their swords into the beastly flesh and ripping it open to reveal a plethora of tiny blue beetles hiding inside.

In an instant, everything was enveloped by a horse cackle as the insects swarmed them, biting and stinging, crawling under their clothes, and trying to burrow under their skin using their sharp mandibles. Keri screamed and started backing away, swinging her sword wildly, trying to swat the insects. Meanwhile, Leonard dropped to the ground, clawing at his skin frantically while bellowing in terror and pain.

With the demonic cackle still echoing around them, the fleshy walls of the chamber burst open, and out of them started crawling creatures with severely disfigured swollen bodies and faces covered with yellowish pustules. They were all shrieking horribly, their voices mixing with the persisting cackling enveloping everything in an infernal cacophony.

Wincing from numerous bites and still flailing frantically with her sword, Keri shifted her eyes to Leonard, squirming on the ground. The man tried to cover his face while wailing hysterically, seemingly teetering on the edge of irremediable madness.

"Leonard, I need your help!" Keri screamed through the raging chaos. However, her words didn't seem to reach the hunter as he cowered while rocking back and forth, as the insects continued picking at his skin.

Meanwhile, the swollen creatures were approaching, extending their pulsating limbs. Still trying to swat the bugs away, Keri stepped forward to meet them. She gripped the sword handle and, with a mighty swing, cut the two closest monsters in half, splattering their guts. She then swung again, taking down three more beasts. However, more of them were quickly approaching.

Keri swung twice, then started coughing as one of the beetles tried to crawl down her throat. She gasped a few times, then sank her teeth into the insect's shell, tasting its sour insides that splattered into her mouth. She then raised her eyes to see that one of the gargling spawns managed to get close.

The beast grabbed Keri by the arm as its body swelled rapidly before exploding, covering her in black mucus and flinging her into the air. Keri gasped as she dropped heavily to the ground, her vision darkening momentarily. She felt her skin burning and heard the beetles screeching in their shared agony.

Somehow, she managed to push off the ground to see Leonard lying a few feet away, with monsters quickly approaching them from all sides. Keri grabbed the man by the arm, pulling it from his face before looking into his frightened eyes. "You got to help me, or we'll be stuck here forever," she said hoarsely. "Remember who you are. Remember what your family once stood for. Grab your sword, and let's send these beasts back to hell."

"My family…" Leonard uttered. Briefly, something flashed in his eyes, and he looked around like he had just awoken from a very long dream.

They got up, clutching their weapons, and started swinging at the approaching horde, drenching the floor with blood, gore, and rancid goo. A few creatures exploded before they could take them down, drenching them with burning liquid and staggering both. However, with combined effort, they managed to slay them all before slumping to the ground, completely exhausted.

They spent several minutes swatting the few remaining beetles, still trying to burrow into their flesh. Finally, when the last insect was dead, they raised their eyes, observing each other's sorry state: they were riddled with deep cuts and gashes, their clothes were turned to shreds, and their skin was blackened from the burns.

"Can you continue like this?" Keri uttered through her clenched teeth, panting, feeling a burning sensation in her lungs.

Leonard nodded. "I'm sorry for what happened. I suppose even death can not cure my innate cowardice." He chuckled faintly, then started coughing, spitting blood and mucus from his mouth.

The fit lasted for a few seconds. When Leonard finally got a hold of himself, he wiped the disgusting mixture from his lips with his sleeve before continuing: "You were right about what you said. While my ancestors were a pompous bunch, for decades, they were the only ones standing between the human world and the eldritch beings of the Beyond. I think I'm finally ready to make peace with that fact."

The man grabbed his sword and pushed off the ground before extending his hand. "I will not be broken anymore," he said. "Let's slay the hag together so I can join my family in eternal rest."

Keri smiled faintly, then took Leonard's hand and rose from the ground. They spent some time looking around the chamber, sloshing through the disgusting sea of gore and pus before they found a narrow round entrance in the back covered with a thin yellow membrane. Keri cut it open and stepped into the damp tunnel riddled with pulsating growths emanating a faint purple light.

They walked for a while as the tunnel slowly descended into the underground. Keri was dragging her feet, wincing from numerous injuries, her burned skin feeling like it was about to peel off her flesh. From occasional grunts, she presumed that Leonard wasn't feeling much better, but still, they kept pushing forward, driven by a determination to escape the cursed domain.

After some time, they felt the ground moving underneath their feet and heard monotonous thudding coming from the distance. Shortly, the tunnel ended, and they stepped into another massive chamber with tall black walls soaked in bluish illumination. At the back, hanging from rippling flesh, was a giant red heart, pumping some black liquid in and out through numerous thick veins. In front of it stood thirteen beings clad in black ragged cloaks.

After Keri and Leonard stepped inside, they all turned, revealing their twisted figures with bones jutting out of their rotten flesh. The ghoulish congregation cackled in unison, their faces contorted with malevolent glee. Then, they extended their hands forward and started chanting ominously in some infernal tongue.

"Don't let them cast the spell!" Keri yelled, then lunged forward with Leonard following behind her.

They got to the center of the chamber when from under the ground, sprouted an amalgamation of quivering roots, instantly wrapping around their legs, locking them in place. Meanwhile, the witches continued to chant, and Keri could see a green mist rising from their mouths and slowly filling the room. She screamed and started cutting through the roots, but more were sprouting from the ground, grabbing and squeezing, slowly creeping toward her neck.

Keri staggered, almost dropping to the ground, suddenly feeling an overwhelming fatigue. Looking at the deadly fumes spreading throughout the chamber, dark thoughts began to arise, questioning the cogency of her struggle. Yet, when she was about to fall, she heard the distant clanging again and felt someone calling out to her from a place many light-years away.

Keri's eyes lit up with the emerald gleam, and she released a thunderous scream that made the roots holding her and Leonard shrivel and retract under the ground. She then glanced back at the hunter before clenching her teeth and rushing forward, feeling the cosmic energy pulsating throughout her flesh.

The witches scattered, avoiding her attacks by shifting through space, their bodies twitching and jerking uncannily. The two closest to Keri leaned forward and released an ear-piercing shriek, making her wobble and momentarily darkening her vision. Seconds later, she felt sharp nails sinking into her flesh, and she turned to see another witch with her hand covered in blood and an uncanny grin hanging on her face.

Keri swiped at the demon with all her might, but it shifted aside, avoiding the massive blade. From the corner of her eye, she saw Leonard dropping to the ground with five witches surrounding him, evading his attacks while scratching his flesh with their sharp nails and cackling maniacally. Keri fixed her gaze on the heart beating at the back of the room with five remaining witches standing before it, continuing to chant and conjuring the green mist that had already reached her waist.

"Go for the heart!" Keri yelled, then started sprinting across the chamber.

The attacking witches immediately retreated, their cackles turning into angry shrieks. Then, they raised their hands, summoning a mighty gust of wind that enveloped Keri and Leonard, lifting the green fumes from the ground and forming a thick cloud that blocked Keri's vision and sent her into a coughing fit. Seconds later, a dozen bony hands emerged from the mist, grabbing her arms and legs and dragging her to the ground. Then, one of the witches leaped from the murk, wrapped her bony fingers around Keri's neck, and started to squeeze.

She struggled to breathe, squirming and trying to sink her teeth into one of the beastly hands, but they kept squeezing her harder, sinking sharp nails into her flesh. Keri felt her spirit rising, and she saw Leonard struggling nearby. She called out to him, looking from above into the man's fading eyes.

Suddenly, the reality shifted, and they saw the long corridors of the Wyrm castle with massive paintings of the beasts hanging on the walls and the statue of the Crimson Watcher standing in the inner courtyard. They also saw the shadows of Leonard's ancestors wandering the halls, heard their wailing whispers, and felt their contempt for all the eldritch creatures that dared to invade their world. Then, they were brought back into the chamber with the foul heart of Heket and its ghoulish protectors. However, they were no longer alone in this fight.

Following a loud crackle, Leonard's flesh parted, splattering blood and gore, and from inside emerged a giant creature with scaly skin and broad leathery wings. The beast turned its massive head and opened its maw, crushing two witches in a single bite. It then pushed off with its talons and leaped forward, with a mighty swipe knocking back the demons holding Keri and setting her free. Briefly, their eyes locked, and she realized what she had to do.

Ignoring many pains surging through her body, Keri jumped to her feet, then leaped on the creature's back. The beast released a thunderous roar and charged at the Heket's heart. The witches tried to stop them, shrieking and casting their spells, but they just bounced off Leonard's scales. Meanwhile, Keri stood up, grasping the greatsword firmly in her hands. She took a deep breath, then ran across the beast's back and leaped from its head, thrusting the massive blade into the center of the pulsating flesh.

The chamber was enveloped by shrieks and bellows as black liquid and yellow pus started to ooze from the massive wound, drenching Keri from head to toe. She staggered, lost her balance, and fell to the ground, then tilted her head to have another look at Leonard's dark eyes before everything faded back into the void.

Sofia

They were trudging with the main road on their right and the Grandlem Mountains on their left. Their journey after leaving Kalenburg was uneventful, apart from a few more thunderous screams that made Sofia's body tremble from fear and agitation. She was always known for her timid nature and was therefore sheltered by her brothers and sisters. Especially Adam and Anabel, who always knew how to soothe her fearful mind.

Since the nightmarish events started, Sofia had been drifting in and out of a dreamlike state, her mind trying desperately to shield itself from the madness that accepting her reality would bring. And only during the past couple hours of ambling silently through the crimson-soaked land, the grim realization dawn on her that perhaps the infernal visions were real. Perhaps Eric and Adam were really dead, Anabel was turned into a monster, and they were being pursued by the demonic creatures intending to devour them alive.

Sofia whimpered, hugging her trembling shoulders. Julie, walking beside her, gave her a quick glance before shifting her gaze back to the tall buildings of Dahbus looming on the horizon, covered with a thick layer of mist.

"We'll need to stay very quiet after we enter the city," Faye said, walking behind them. "If we see even a hint of the beasts, we'll go around and head for Kebury."

"And what if the port is also overrun?" Julie asked.

"Then we'll find a boat and get the hell out of this continent."

"But isn't the sea where that horrible sound is coming from?" Sofia whimpered.

Both women looked at her, seeming surprised since she had been silent for hours.

"Maybe we should head to the Capital," Sofia continued. "That's where the military would be if they're still alive."

"If they're still alive, they're probably surrounded by those things," Faye argued. "Otherwise, they'd already be here. Of course, you two can do whatever you want, but I'm getting on that boat and sailing to Talos."

"I agree with Faye," Julie said. "We have no idea what the actual source of the sound is. All we know is that Orox is under attack, and it would be wise to get as far away from the continent as possible."

"What if the same is happening in Talos?" Sofia asked.

"Well, then we're done for anyways," Faye grumbled. "Might as well take the chance." She sighed, then got a bit closer while raising her shotgun. "Now enough chatter, we don't know how sensitive to sound those monsters are."

Sofia pressed the sword handle to her chest and took a deep breath while peering fearfully at the murky outskirts of Dahbus outstretching before them. She felt her heart pounding, and her breathing now seemed incredibly loud in the eerie tranquility hanging over the city.

Soon, they stepped onto the paved road and started ambling through the empty streets, looking around for any signs of life. However, the only things they encountered so far were a few wrecked cars and puddles of some black slime, exuding the most putrid odor that Sofia had ever smelled. She covered her nose with her wrist, turning her head away and trying not to gag.

Suddenly, she felt someone grabbing her arm, and she turned to see Julie, with her eyes wide, pointing at something ahead. Feeling her teeth beginning to chatter, Sofia gazed in that direction to see some twitchy figure standing in the mist.

They started backing away. Meanwhile, the being turned and began shambling in their direction, making creepy guttural clicks. Soon, it stepped into the light of one of the flashing lampposts, exposing its bizarre frame with long lanky legs, a fat belly, and a twisted neck branching into three wrinkled heads. From each of those heads, a single bloodshot eye leered at the three women, and Sofia could now also see tiny mouths underneath biting at the air with sharp little teeth.

The monster stood still for a few seconds, staring at them intently. Then, it released an ear-piercing shriek and charged forward, flailing numerous quivering limbs sticking out of its torso.

Sofia released a fearful gasp and raised her trembling hands, clutching the sword. Meanwhile, Faye stepped forward, aimed her shotgun, and fired at the approaching beast. The pellets pierced the monster's flesh, and it staggered, taking a step back. But then, it shrieked again and resumed its attack, splattering thick blood along the way.

Faye fired two more times, the last shot clipping one of the monster's heads, which exploded in a cloud of gore. Gargling, the creature slumped to the ground and began twitching with blood pouring from numerous gunshot wounds.

"Let's get out of here," Faye said while reloading her shotgun.

They were about to go back the way they came when everything was enveloped by ghastly howls that froze the blood in Sofia's veins. Then, from the dark alleyways, hairy wolflike beasts began emerging, leering at the women with their bulging yellow eyes. Growling and barking, they quickly encircled them and started approaching while brandishing their claws and gnashing their fangs.

The women were looking desperately for any escape routes. But unfortunately, the beasts were crawling from every direction, some even climbing from windows and balconies of the surrounding buildings.

Suddenly, the closest monster leaped forward, extending its claws, but it was immediately brought down by another blast of Faye's shotgun. As the creature dropped to the ground, the remaining wolfmen resumed howling, baring their fangs, seemingly preparing to attack. Meanwhile, more of them were coming, quickly filling the streets with hairy bodies.

"Over here, quick!" Faye shouted, her voice trembling. She rushed to the nearby two-story lodge and kicked its door open before leaping inside. Julie and Sofia followed behind while the wolfmen, after another series of howls, rushed forward, beginning their assault.

Seconds after the women slammed the door shut and leaned their backs against it, they felt the beasts pounding and scraping on the other side, trying to get in.

"Help me move this thing!" Faye shouted, grabbing onto a large shelf standing by the door. With a combined effort, they tilted it over before stepping aside and letting it fall, trapping the head of one of the wolfmen who managed to peek inside.

The beast began barking and growling, trying to squeeze the rest of its body through. Meanwhile, Julie stepped forward and stabbed the creature's eye with a sword that pierced its flesh like butter, splattering blood on the woman's face. The wolfman whimpered and withdrew, allowing them to close the door and push the fallen shelf closer, preventing the beasts from coming in.

Sofia was about to breathe a sigh of relief when she heard the glass shattering on the second floor, followed by the scampering of the beastly feet. Seconds later, two wolfmen emerged atop the narrow staircase leading into the hallway. At the same time, she heard another glass shattering at the back of the house.

Faye raised her shotgun and fired, sending one of the beasts on the stairs backward. She then turned and ran out of the hallway. Julie and Sofia followed her into a small room with a single bed, a large closet, and a tiny window. After shutting the door, Faye shoved the bed against it while Julie and Sofia pushed the closet in front of the window, barricading themselves in.

Finally, breathing heavily, all three slumped in the middle of the room, listening to the beasts howling and barking outside. The door trembled several times as something big smashed at it from the other side before releasing an angry growl. Then abruptly, everything fell silent.

After exchanging fearful glances with Julie and Faye, Sofia noticed something dripping on the floor, and she tilted her head to see blood seeping from the large gash on her sister's arm. "Julie, you're hurt," Sofia whimpered.

Her sister lowered her eyes, looking at the grisly wound. "Oh, I didn't even notice when I got it."

"It probably happened when you stabbed the beast trying to get inside," Faye said, then extended her hand, grabbed a white sheet from the bed, and tore a big piece off before handing it to Julie. "Here, patch yourself up."

With Sofia's help, Julie bandaged her wound, stopping the bleeding. She then leaned her back against the wall and sighed. "What now?"

"Now we'll wait for the beasts to leave," Faye uttered, then sat on the bed and put the shotgun on her lap. "Then, we'll sneak out of the house, escape the town and continue to Kebury."

"How will we know that they left?" Sofia asked, looking fearfully at the barricaded doors.

Faye shrugged. "We'll just have to assume. In the meantime, we should take this opportunity to get some rest. There's still a long road ahead of us."

Eliza

Eliza sat in the corner, her eyes fixed on Daniel lying limply in the other cell. The man hadn't moved since the seizure he had, and she feared the worst. She tried calling the guards, but no one came, and her pleas were only answered by the monstrous screams that were now becoming more frequent. Thus, she eventually gave up and, for a while now, sat silently while gnawing on her lips with her teeth, many of which were cracked in her fight against Fenrir. She hoped that the pain would help her stay awake, but she could already feel her mind drifting into the dark.

"Get a hold of yourself," Eliza muttered. "You can't fall asleep now when there's no knowing what would happen next."

She got up, shambled to the bars, and tried speaking to Daniel again, but the man still lay unmovingly, drool seeping from his mouth. "God damn it!" Eliza cried out and pulled several times on the bars, but they didn't budge. She was about to return to her corner when she heard a distant rustle.

"Hello?!" she exclaimed, peering at the door on the other side of the room. Shortly, the rustling came back, this time a bit closer. "Hey! We need help down here!" Eliza yelled. "We need—" she stopped mid-sentence, recognizing the footsteps of webbed slimy feet. The sound she got accustomed to while living in the underground as the Queen of Depth.

Eliza withdrew and returned to the corner, her body trembling from fear. "No," she whimpered. "I escaped that place. Keri freed me from Dagon's curse. So… just leave me alone!"

The footsteps were coming closer. In Eliza's mind arose the images of grotesque fishmen, followed by the vision of Dagon sitting on his throne, staring at her with dead black eyes. She could already smell the pungent stench of mold, rot, and decay, and she started gagging and dry-heaving, feeling her empty stomach contracting painfully.

Eliza saw the shadow outstretching from the doorway, and she screamed in desperation, pressing her back to the cold wall as the being stepped into the dim light of the ceiling lamp. However, it was not the fishman or any other beast but a woman wearing a long black cloak. She walked to the middle of the room, then turned her head to Eliza and smiled broadly from her pale face framed by long blonde hair.

"You!" Eliza exclaimed, feeling shivers running down her spine. "I shot you! I saw you fade away!"

"Hello, Eliza," Sila chirped. "So nice to see you after all that time."

Eliza looked around, clenching her teeth, as if to make sure there wasn't some hidden passageway leading out of her cell that she somehow missed. Meanwhile, Sila took a step closer and continued: "I come bearing a gift, my dear. One that would allow you to break your shackles and save Keri from her suffering."

Eliza widened her eyes. "Keri? Is she in the palace? Is she still alive?"

"Barely." Sila took another step forward and leaned toward the bars, continuing to smile, her white teeth glinting in the twilight. "At this moment, she's being tortured, just like your buddy Daniel was. And I'm afraid that with her injuries, she doesn't have much time left. Unless you embrace the power that I'm so graciously willing to bestow upon you."

"You're a liar, demon," Eliza uttered. "I don't know what you're trying to achieve by talking to me, but I have no intention of believing a single word coming from your foul mouth!"

Sila chuckled. "Oh, dear, what did I ever do to you to deserve such hostility? Well, you may not believe my words, but what if you saw it with your own eyes?"

The woman extended her pale hand and snapped her fingers. In an instant, the cell disappeared, and Eliza found herself standing in a small dark room. Keri was shackled to the wall in front, blood dripping from her battered face. Her gory stump was flailing frantically while the man dressed in a dark-blue suit beat her mercilessly, smashing her face and torso with his fists.

"Keri!" Eliza screamed and rushed forward.

The vision faded, and she slammed into the bars of her cell, then staggered backward before slumping to the ground, gasping. She tilted her head, looking at Sila's smiling visage, feeling tears welling in her eyes.

"So how about it?" the witch asked. "Do you believe me now?"

"No," Eliza whimpered, then grabbed her head with her hands and started rocking back and forth. "Just leave me alone. If you actually wanted to help, you would let us out of these cages."

"Oh, but I want to help." Sila sighed. "It's just that my help doesn't come for free. There's something I need you to do first."

"I'm not doing anything for you."

Eliza tried to cover her ears, but she could still hear Sila's voice in her head. "You were marked by the Deep One, and although you have severed your connection, you still bear his curse. Along with it comes the power to open the gates to the obsidian waste and beckon the Shadow of Dagon into your realm."

"I won't do it," Eliza whimpered.

"Open the gates, call your infernal army as the Queen of the Deep, and claim this world for yourself before the beast devours it whole. This is the only way, dear Eliza. The only way you can save your beloved Keri and the rest of the world."

"You're a liar!" Eliza screamed, then jumped to her feet, intending to reach through the bars and grab the witch's neck.

She was met by the bright-emerald gleam coming from Sila's eye socket that was previously covered with an eye patch. Eliza felt herself falling as the cell disappeared again, giving way to the boundless darkness filled with strange whispers speaking in languages she had never heard before.

Eliza felt her essence stretching, and she screamed in fear, raising her hands, trying to grasp the empty space to prevent herself from falling apart. Then suddenly, she felt a solid surface under her feet, and she staggered, teetering on the edge of the steep cliff with nothing but an expanse of pitch-blackness looming below.

Breathing heavily, Eliza stepped back, then turned to see hordes of fishmen gathered in the obsidian waste soaked in purple illumination. In front of them stood Dagon himself, towering over his spawns, his dark eyes peering at her intently. The beast released a hoarse gargle, then stepped forward, extending his scaly claw riddled with disgusting pulsating blisters. Eliza recoiled, stepping back to the edge before looking over her shoulder, deliberating whether she should plunge into the murky dark.

As she hesitated, she felt the monster grabbing her by the arm and yanking her forward. Eliza fell to the ground, then tilted her head to sea Dagon hunched over her, baring his sharp fangs, rancid yellow mucus seeping from his mouth. She screamed, then tried to get up, but the beast pinned her to the ground, continuing to leer into her eyes.

Eliza heard his infernal voice again, commanding her to accept her fate, and she felt the demon's desire to leave the black waste and conquer the human world. Then, she saw billions of fishmen marching, armed with primitive weaponry, burning towns and taking people captive to be later devoured or turned to join the Dagon's army.

"Open the gates, Eliza," she heard Sila whisper. "This is your purpose. There's no other way."

She screamed, then started squirming, trying to get free, but the demonic grip was just getting tighter, sharp nails digging into her chest and her ribs cracking from pressure.

"Just let go," Sila continued. "It will all be over once you give in. No more pain or anguish – just an empty void unburdened by petty thoughts."

Eliza shrieked in dismay and anger, directed at all the eldritch beings she had encountered that took her away from her peaceful existence in Exter. That followed her all the way to Orox when she just wished to hide in the mountains and slowly whittle away in her beastly form. All those twisted demons who wanted to use her to fulfill their wicked ambitions.

"Leave me alone!" Eliza screamed. "You can kill me if you want, but I'll never serve you again! Not you, not anyone else in this miserable world!"

Suddenly, something changed. A beam of bright light pierced through the purple skies. Then, following a loud bang, Dagon's head exploded, splattering Eliza's face with a disgusting mixture of blood, mucus, and gore.

The demonic grip loosened, and the creature collapsed to the ground. Eliza got up, gagging and gasping, then shifted her eyes to see a burly man with a lush mustache standing about fifty yards away, holding a massive rifle. Meanwhile, angry barks and gargles broke throughout the field as the horde of fishmen rushed to protect their master.

Holding onto her aching ribs, Eliza started running toward the man who saved her. He waited until she got closer, then turned and took off, avoiding numerous spears and daggers flying his way.

They ran through the obsidian waste for a while, moving away from the edge and leaving the army of fishmen behind them. When they finally stopped, Eliza collapsed, completely drained, then started coughing while spitting blood from her mouth.

"We can not linger for long," she heard the man's deep husky voice.

Eliza widened her eyes, and her heart fluttered painfully in her chest. She raised her head to see Chief Walter standing beside her, peering at her with his penetrating brown eyes. "Walter," she whimpered, then pushed off the ground and stepped forward, wrapping her arms around the man's neck.

They stood like this for some time before Walter withdrew, his eyes fixed on the dark silhouettes moving on the horizon. "They're coming," he uttered. "We need to keep going."

The man turned and started walking quickly, and Eliza followed beside him, trying to ignore the stinging sensation in her chest. "Are you really here?" she asked. "What happened? We wanted to look for you, but then all the hell broke loose, and we assumed that you… That you…" Eliza rubbed her nose nervously, then lowered her eyes.

"I was whisked away by the shadows of my past and demonic voices echoing in my head," Walter said. "I ran, then I fell, through time and space, through darkness and void, until nothing of me was left. Just an idea drifting in the hollow. But then, I saw the white light, and I was brought to this place and instructed to wait until you showed up."

"Instructed by whom?" Eliza asked, widening her eyes.

"That I do not know. I was only told to help you get out of this realm."

Eliza pressed her lips tightly, thinking while looking at the strange jagged shapes emerging in the distance. In her mind's eye arose all the good times she had with the Chief and his buddy Edgar while working in Exter's police station. Eliza also remembered their fights caused by her occasional drinking binges. "I'm sorry," she mumbled. "For all the trouble I had caused you guys."

Walter glanced at her, then smirked faintly. "I never held it against you. We were going stir-crazy before you came along. Thus, despite occasional hiccups, we loved having you around."

Eliza smiled. She felt her eyes tremble, longing for the long-lost days. "Back then, all I could think of was fleeing into the wider world," she said. "The first thing I did when I met Keri was ask her to take me back to the city."

Walter raised his eyebrows. "Oh? You should've told me. I didn't know that you were this unhappy."

Eliza shook her head. "No. It was on me. I didn't know what I wanted, but I now understand that my need to escape your supervision was partly led by the desire to start using again. After everything I went through, I realize that the years I spent with you guys were the happiest in my life."

Walter gave her an intent look, then averted his gaze before muttering: "I see. I'm glad."

The distant shapes were becoming clearer, reminding Eliza slightly of the monoliths she saw in the mountains where they fought the monstrous wolf Fenrir. "Where are we going?" she asked.

"Toward the gateway."

Eliza widened her eyes. "Gateway?" she repeated, feeling shivers running down her spine.

What if this is one of Sila's tricks?

"Won't Dagon and his army follow us?" she asked.

"I'll stay behind and make sure they don't."

Eliza's eyes trembled again. She extended her hand, grabbed the man by the sleeve, then stopped, looking at him intently. Walter also stopped and turned, then gave her another gloomy smirk. "It's okay. My spirit is already lost to the land of the living. After I'm done here, I'll just return to the void."

"But—"

"It's okay. I was weak. And I still am. I wouldn't be able to keep my sanity for long, knowing the evil that lurks in the cosmos."

A single tear escaped Eliza's eye and rolled down her cheek. "What makes you think I can handle those demons any better?" she whimpered. "I want to go with you. I want to fade away into the dark."

"You're a lot stronger than you think. Just remember all the hardships you went through. First, you beat your addiction, then you overcame the Dagon's curse, and you even resisted the temptations of the witch. Few could've kept their mind and spirit from breaking after experiencing such unspeakable horrors."

Eliza released Walter's sleeve and lowered her eyes, tears rolling down her face.

"Besides, Keri needs you," Walter continued. "She's the only one who can save our world. And you're the most important person in her life."

Eliza raised her gaze. Her heart trembled as Keri's tired visage arose from the darkness of her mind. "The being that brought you here told you all this?" she asked.

Walter nodded, then resumed his amble toward the rock formations glinting in the distance. Eliza hesitated, then looked over her shoulder at the hordes of fishmen slowly shambling toward them. She also saw Dagon walking in the back, already recovered from his injuries.

Eliza sighed deeply, then turned and caught up to Walter. They walked the rest of the way in silence. Eliza kept glancing over her shoulder at the ghoulish creatures following them, her heart beating heavily in her aching chest and dark thoughts rising in her mind.

If Sila somehow got into my head, she definitely could've conjured Walter's apparition to trick me into opening the gates. Therefore, I must be very careful about what I do next.

They stepped into the field surrounded by thirteen tall monoliths, their sharp edges glinting eerily in the purple illumination. Eliza glanced again at the monsters shambling in the distance before fixing her eyes on Walter. "Why are they not rushing us?" she asked.

"They're waiting for you to open the gates," the Chief said, then motioned toward the circle of tiny white rocks in the middle of the field. "Stand over there and stay very still."

"How will you stop them?"

"I'm not sure. We'll just have to trust the powers that brought me here."

"What if the same powers that pulled you out of the void want Dagon to enter our world? What if we're being played?"

Walter frowned, seemingly thinking deeply, then shook his head. "No, that is not possible. The voice that spoke to me was the opposite of the infernal tongue I heard while plummeting to my death. It belonged to the prideful ethereal entity as old as the universe itself. It would never lower itself as to walk among the mortals."

"Prideful?" Eliza raised her eyebrows.

"We don't have time. They are getting closer."

Walter pushed her lightly, then gripped his rifle and turned around, looking at the approaching army. Eliza hesitated a bit longer, then, on shaky legs, walked to the middle of the stone circle. Nothing happened at first, but then, she felt energy surging through her body, and she saw the black monoliths beginning to glisten. At the same time, dozens of shrieks came from the distance as the beasts started their charge.

Walter turned to Eliza, giving her one more smile, then got on one knee and started blasting at the monsters from his rifle. Meanwhile, the air thickened, and she heard a sickening hum that quickly became louder, drilling into her brain and making her temples throb painfully.

Eliza grabbed her head and hunched her back, with her dimming gaze looking at Walter clutching his rifle by the barrel and swinging it like a sword at the fishmen trying to get through. Then, she saw Dagon's massive figure leaning over and grabbing the man, intending to throw him aside. But just as the beast's hand touched Walter's skin, Chief's body shattered into pieces, sending a massive shock wave that toppled the beasts, pushing them away from the stone circle. At the same time, the entire field was engulfed by a white light, and a few seconds later, everything was over.

Abruptly, Eliza was thrust back into her tiny cell. She quickly looked around, expecting to see Sila or maybe even the entire ghoulish army crawling from a gap in space. However, there was nothing.

She breathed a sigh of relief, then stepped back and sat in the corner of her cell, still frightened but also hopeful. She pondered about what Walter said: that some ethereal being was trying to help them in this fight. Then, her thoughts shifted, and she saw Keri's face again, floating in the darkness of her mind.

Eliza clasped her hands, closed her eyes, and started praying for the spirits of the fallen and those still struggling in the battle that would determine the fate of their world.

Kyron

Kyron saw himself standing on a short hill overlooking the town of Lerwick. The remnants of the rebel army were fleeing the mountains, chased by his loyal troops. He grabbed his trusted rifle from his back and looked through the scope at the young man running with his eyes full of terror. Then, without hesitation, he pushed the trigger and saw the man's brains splatter before he slumped to the ground, his mouth wide open and his eyes now empty, staring back at Kyron in the look of utmost anguish that would end up haunting his dreams for the decades to come.

Kyron shuddered and woke up to excruciating pain pulsating in his flesh. He gasped a few times and tried to move, but all he could muster was a slight twitch of his fingers. With his heart pounding, he gazed blindly at the jumble of color and shadow wavering before him. Slowly, the shapes began to appear, forming a visage of a man he once knew. Kyron saw his lips moving but could not yet make out the words through the loud hum in his ears. Then finally, a few phrases broke through the veil of pain and dizziness: "Kyron? Kyron, can you hear me?"

"Where am I?" he uttered hoarsely, then coughed a few times, the pain in his lungs briefly becoming insufferable.

The world disappeared again. When Kyron returned, he finally recalled that the man leaning over him was Major Daley of the Intercontinental Military Force. He also remembered their perilous mission and the horrible monsters that attacked them.

Kyron turned his head slightly to see that Major's midsection was heavily bandaged. Then, he gasped a few times before muttering: "How are the things in the city?"

"About half of the troops managed to return behind the walls," Daley said. "Demonic swarm attacked several apartment buildings and a hospital, but we managed to push them back."

"What about the giant?"

"The beast retreated after suffering several shots from our tank."

Kyron tried to move again but only managed to lift several of his fingers.

"You should rest," Daley said, seeing the struggle on his face.

"I'm done for, aren't I?"

"We have the best available staff working on you, so—"

"Don't give me that nonsense," Kyron grumbled, then coughed several times before clenching his teeth after another surge of excruciating pain.

Daley looked at him for a bit longer, then sighed and said: "I'm afraid it doesn't look good."

"Take good care of my people, okay? Kill every single one of those cursed fiends and rebuild our land."

"I'll do my best, Sir," the Major said, then put his hand on Kyron's shoulder before finally turning and exiting the main ward of the Royal Palace.

After he left, Kyron closed his eyes and started waiting for death's cold embrace to take him while concentrating all his remaining strength on pushing back the feelings of anguish and self-pity that tried to arise from his fading mind. But the death lingered, and the pain kept rising, making him grunt and gasp, fading in and out of consciousness. At one point, he felt something slimy touch his body, which was followed by a sharp piercing sensation. Then, he finally drifted into the dark, abandoning all his hopes and aspirations.

For a while, Kyron stopped existing as a person, and only a vague idea of him floated between the looms of times. But then, something moved in the void, making him regain his sense of self. His memories also came back, along with the vision of a boundless wasteland of rough crimson rock. Then, he saw himself standing before him with a face distorted by a creepy grin.

"Great Kyron, so easily defeated by the mindless beasts," his apparition said in a hoarse echoey voice. "Once so mighty, you grew complaisant playing your political games, sitting cozily in the Royal Palace."

"Who are you?" the man muttered.

"I am the blackest abyss of the universe. I reside in the shadow of the cosmos. And now, I came to you bearing a gift – an opportunity to wield the power of the gods and use it to banish the evil from your land."

Kyron widened his eyes. "You can help me defeat the monsters?"

"The beasts you've faced pale compared to the enemy that rises from the sea, the insatiable maw that wants to devour your world. You heard it scream many times under the blood moon."

"I'll do anything to save my people," Kyron uttered through clenched teeth, anger rising for the otherworldly forces that invaded *his* world.

The entity extended its hand while tilting its head to the side. "Then take my hand, the great ruler of Orox. Claim this gift and all the knowledge that comes with it."

Kyron started lifting his arm, then stopped midway, doubt suddenly arising in his mind. "Why are you helping me?"

"Because you're special, Kyron, and you, more than anyone, are the most deserving of this gift. Still, you are free to choose whether to claim this power and banish the demons from your world. Or, you could refuse and return to the void where you would be soon joined by the rest of your kin."

Kyron pressed his lips tightly, thinking. While the being before him looked exactly like him, something about how it moved and talked made the uneasiness grow within. Somewhere, at the back of his mind, a tiny voice was screaming at him, telling him to refuse the temptation and embrace the shadows. However, in the end, his pride and lust for power overcame his fear, making him extend his arm and shake the creature's hand.

Christa

Christa and Darren stood beside Nina, lying in bed in the small private ward on the first floor of the hospital building. The soldiers were walking back and forth outside, and they could hear the sobs and moans of the people injured during the demon attack, along with those mourning their fallen loved ones.

Darren leaned closer to Christa and muttered: "I better get going. Will you be okay on your own?"

She widened her eyes. "You still want to go? Those beasts may be scattered all over the city. Furthermore, it'll be a hundred times more difficult to sneak into the palace with all the soldiers back inside the walls."

Darren glanced at the open doorway where a tall uniformed man was walking past. He then shifted his eyes back to Christa. "I actually think the opposite is true," he said. "With all this commotion, there will be plenty of opportunity to slip past. Also, I heard that something might've happened to Kyron, so the guards will be focused on protecting him rather than watching the prisoners."

Christa pressed her lips tightly. While she didn't want to be left alone, she worried greatly about what may happen to Daniel and Keri. "I suppose you're right," she muttered after a short pause, then looked at Nina. "But what should I do about her? Should I tell someone what happened?"

Darren shook his head. "We have no idea what happened. Or if it can happen again. Better not to speculate and keep it a secret – if you told the soldiers, they would surely take her away."

Christa lowered her eyes, thinking. Meanwhile, Darren stepped closer and placed his hand on her shoulder. "Take care of yourself. Hopefully, we'll meet again in the aftermath of this hell."

They looked into each other's eyes a bit longer. Then, Darren lifted his collar, turned, and exited the room. After he left, Christa sighed, turned her attention back to Nina, and started slowly stroking the girl's curly black hair. Looking at Nina's pale visage, she found herself wondering about all the horrors she had experienced during the past month. Once again, tears started welling in her eyes after the faces of her friends and family arose in her mind. Deep inside, Christa still clung to the hope that they might've avoided the plague that ravaged the Kradena Port, turning all its inhabitants into horrific beasts.

Perhaps they managed to flee the city when it started and now reside somewhere in the Heart of Talos. Hopefully, the things over there aren't as dire as they are here.

"In any case, at least I still have you, little one," Christa said, then sighed and lowered her eyes while pressing her hand to her lips, trying to push back the rising sob.

She stood still for a bit, her shoulders shaking slightly while thinking about the grimness of her situation. Then, after regaining her composure, she wiped tears from her eyes and glanced back at Nina before releasing a surprised gasp.

The girl's big blue eyes were wide open, staring vacantly at the ceiling. Christa extended her shaking hand and gently touched her shoulder. "Nina? Can you hear me?"

The girl lay still for a few uneasy seconds, then turned her head, opened her mouth, and muttered hoarsely: "Miss Christa?"

Christa gasped again, raising her hand to her mouth. Meanwhile, Nina pushed off with her hands and sat up. Then, she took a few deep breaths, lifted her feet out of bed, and tried to stand up, but her legs gave out. She was about to tumble to the floor, but Christa grabbed her at the last moment, then helped her to sit back down before asking: "Where are you going, dear?"

"I need to go to Keri," Nina said, looking at Christa intently. "I need to make sure she's safe."

"Darren went out to rescue her, dear. So, you have nothing to fear."

"I need to go to her," Nina insisted, then tried to stand up again, but Christa didn't let her, placing her hands on the girl's shoulders.

"Nina, do you remember what happened a few hours ago? Do you remember waking up?"

The girl pouted her lower lip, then shook her head. "I need to go," she repeated, tears welling in her eyes.

"But why? Are you not afraid of the monsters?"

"I am," Nina said, then lowered her eyes. "But… Miss Keri is suffering. She's fighting very hard to save us. We need to protect her so she can come back."

"Come back?" Christa raised her eyebrows. "Nina, what are you talking about?"

"The lady in white told me to look out for her. So, please, Miss Christa, let me go!"

Nina fixed her tearful gaze on Christa again as the woman tried her hardest to grasp what she was hearing. She was fairly certain that the girl's desire to find Keri was fueled by the delusion induced by her comatose state. However, she could not dismiss Nina's claims entirely because of what happened during the demon attack.

Some external force was definitely manifesting through this child.

However, that doesn't mean it's still inside her. I can't let her go out there when so many things are uncertain.

"Why don't we take a few minutes to think it through?" Christa said. "In the meantime, tell me more about this lady in white. Did you see her in a dream?"

"We don't have time," Nina whimpered, then turned her head, her eyes suddenly becoming very wide.

"Nina, what's wrong?"

"It's already here," the girl whispered, looking at the doorway.

Christa felt shivers running down her spine. "What do you mean?"

The girl twitched, and the corner of her lip sagged uncannily. Then, she opened her mouth and uttered hoarsely: "It is named the Carrion Hoarder by the void, and it shambles through the broken seams, collecting the corpses of the dead and dragging them into the carrion pits where they're devoured by the foul and the corrupted." Nina inhaled deeply, producing a creepy wheeze, then continued: "It is accompanied by the three-headed demons carrying the name of the Flesh Seekers. Together, they serve the Chaos in exchange for eternal life, and a curse befalls all who cross their path."

Nina wheezed again, then blinked several times before looking around, seeming scared and confused. With her heart pounding, Christa opened her mouth to ask the girl whether she understood what just came out of her mouth. Then suddenly, the building shook violently, sending plaster and dust down from the ceiling. Seconds later, they heard a thunderous bellow, followed by a sharp crack of gunshots and numerous panicked screams.

"We need to get out of here!" Christa yelled, then grabbed Nina into her hands and rushed out of the room.

The corridor was crammed with frightened people. Several soldiers tried to aid their retreat while the remaining troops rushed toward the sound. Christa joined the fleeing crowd, looking around nervously. Everyone was pushing each other, trying to get out of the building as soon as possible. Meanwhile, the gunshots and demonic bellows were quickly approaching, echoing throughout the halls.

The exit was already in sight when, following another violent tremble, the wall behind them parted, and a gargantuan abomination emerged from the rubble. The monster released a horrendous howl and started rampaging through the crowd, ignoring the avalanche of bullets battering its flesh and crushing people under its massive elephant feet.

Screaming, the crowd rushed forward, desperate to get out of the building. Christa got pushed into a small corner, unable to move an inch, taking short panicky breaths while watching the beast quickly approaching, leaving piles of corpses in its path. The creature turned its disproportionately small head, its beady eyes momentarily locking with Christa's. It then lunged toward her, extending its massive hands. She shrieked, trying to get out of the way while pressing Nina to her chest.

Suddenly, when the monster was just yards away, its head exploded in a cloud of gory mess. The creature dropped to the ground, and Christa saw a short man with blonde hair standing behind it, holding a smoking rifle.

With the beast down and people pouring out of the crumbling building, Christa finally got out of the corner and left through the door. Outside, she was presented with the ghastly sight of streets splattered with blood and laden with demon and soldier corpses.

"They're coming, Miss Christa," Nina whimpered, then raised her arm, pointing at the large gap in the wall shrouded by a thick mist. Seconds later, following a jumble of infernal shrieks and screeches, ghoulish three-headed creatures started pouring into the inner city, charging at the crowd while flailing their numerous quivering limbs protruding from their pale torsos.

Several soldiers started shooting, but they quickly got overwhelmed. With horror, Christa watched the demons grabbing people and dragging them into the fog while the three heads were biting them with their tiny mouths filled with sharp fangs. She turned and started rushing toward the city center, trying not to trip over the numerous bodies lying in the streets.

Christa parted from the main crowd, stepped into the dark alleyway between two apartment buildings, and continued running while looking around fearfully. She noticed that many windows were shattered, and shards of glass were scattered on the ground, crunching eerily under her feet.

Suddenly, from the darkness of one of the apartments on the first floor, a red-skinned demon with large horns leaped into the open. It smashed into Christa, making her drop Nina and tumble on the pavement, bits of glass cutting the skin of her hands. Gasping, she raised her head to see the monster hunched over her, baring its fangs. She could see disgusting pustules on its skin filled with rancid goo and could smell the stench of death coming from its maw.

"Nina, run!" Christa screamed while looking at the beast's wide eyes emanating a purple gleam.

The demon growled, then raised its claws, intending to rip Christa to shreds. She raised her arms, cowering and bracing herself for her inevitable demise. Then suddenly, she heard Nina's scream, and moments later, the demon was lifted into the air by some invisible force before being smashed into the wall.

Christa got up, looking at the emerald light emanating from the girl's eyes. Nina whimpered, then wobbled before slumping to the ground. Christa rushed forward, knelt beside her, and took the girl into her arms. Moments later, she heard an angry growl and looked over her shoulder to see the demon slowly getting up, dazed from the collision with the wall but otherwise unscathed.

Clenching her teeth, Christa got up and started running as fast as she could, leaving the alley and continuing toward the city center, trying to stay away from screams and gunfire coming from all directions. Shortly, she stopped in a shadow of a tall red-brick building, panting and looking around, trying desperately to find someplace safe. However, after the last encounter, all the ajar doors and shattered windows gave rise to the imagery of horrible beasts lurking in the shadows.

"I need to go to Keri," Nina muttered. Her eyelids trembled and opened slightly. She then took a deep breath and added: "Miss Christa, please, take me to her."

Christa looked at the little girl, then turned her gaze to the silhouette of the massive Royal Palace looming in the distance. Her eyes widened after seeing three demons circling its spires. She shook her head, then mumbled: "No. It's too dangerous. I need to keep you safe."

Christa was about to start creeping away when she heard a loud growl. She tilted her head to see the same demon that attacked them hanging from the balcony, its face distorted by a ravenous grin. The beast growled again, then dropped down and rushed forward, brandishing its claws.

Christa gasped, then turned and started running. She only managed to take a few steps when sharp nails sank into her back, sending excruciating pain throughout her flesh and making her tumble to the ground. Gasping, still holding Nina pressed against her chest, Christa started kicking with her legs, trying to push the beast away, looking into its gleaming purple eyes, full of nothing but otherworldly malice.

Suddenly, with a loud bang, the demon's chest burst open. Then followed two more shots, taking out part of the creature's face and shattering its left shoulder. Gargling, the beast dropped to the ground, some of its blood splattering on Christa's legs. Meanwhile, she raised her eyes to see Darren running toward her, grasping a pistol in his hand.

The man helped her get up, then grabbed her by the arm and started leading her away from the downed beast, still gargling and squirming on the ground. "The others must've heard the shots," Darren said. "We need to get to the palace while the chaos still rages around us."

"But the demons..." Christa muttered fearfully, pointing at the creatures soaring in the crimson skies.

"I'm not leaving without Daniel," Darren said firmly. "However, I can't stop you from fleeing if that's what you want. Although, at this point, I think it would be safer for you two to stick with me."

"Please, Miss Christa," Nina whimpered, opening her eyes, which made Darren flinch.

"She awoke shortly after you left," Christa explained.

Darren glanced at the girl, then shifted his gaze back to the woman. "So, what will it be?"

Christa glanced at the demons circling the palace before looking into Nina's pleading eyes while trying desperately to come up with the safest course of action.

Apart from Nina's ability, we're defenseless against those monsters. Thus, we're probably better off sticking with Darren. Especially since he had already saved our lives on more than one occasion. If we rescue Daniel and Keri, we might have a shot at escaping the city.

"All right," she said. "We're going with you."

Daley

With his eyes wide, Major Daley watched the giant abomination's flesh ripple, mending itself back together. He ordered ten remaining troops to attack several more times, but nothing they did could finish the beast.

Gritting his teeth, Daley grabbed the radio hanging by his waist. "We need heavy explosives in the hospital, over," he shouted into the device. He waited for a few seconds, then repeated the command but didn't get any response.

Daley was about to order his troops to attack the twitching monster again when suddenly, a soldier emerged at the main entrance. Half his face was ripped open, and his left arm sagged limply from his shoulder. "The wall has been breached!" he hollered. "The monsters are attacking the civilians." The man took a few more steps forward before collapsing. Seconds later, three-headed beasts started pouring into the building.

"Open fire!" Daley yelled, then raised his rifle and started shooting.

Many creatures dropped to the ground, their flesh mangled by bullets. However, their numbers kept growing, and they were slowly pushing forward. Daley saw two beasts grabbing the injured soldier with their ghoulish limbs before dragging him out of the building as he screamed in stark terror.

"Continue firing!" the Major shouted. "Start backing away! Slowly!" He raised the radio to his mouth again and pressed the button, intending to call for backup, when from the device came an ear-piercing screech that only added to the nightmare raging around them.

Daley cursed, dropped the radio, and stomped on it with his foot. He then resumed firing at the approaching monstrous horde. The bodies continued to pile as new beasts kept appearing, screeching horribly and moving in uncanny, jerky motions, trying to avoid the bullets flying their way. The giant abomination was also starting to get up while covering its head with its massive right hand. Meanwhile, Daley and the soldiers were approaching the wall where the corridor branched in two directions.

"Let's move toward the back door in the northern block," the Major commanded.

"Sir, I'm almost out of ammunition!" one of the soldiers shouted.

"I'm also almost out," another soldier concurred.

Daley gritted his teeth, then looked down and saw that only a single box of pistol ammo was left hanging on his vest. He then shifted his gaze to the giant beast that was starting to slowly shamble toward them, accompanied by the continuous wave of three-headed monsters.

"Alright, new plan!" Daley yelled. "On the count of three, throw your grenades, and let's retreat through the back." He grabbed a grenade from his belt, took a deep breath, then counted: "One… Two… Three!"

Eleven grenades soared through the air. Daley and his troops turned, then fled to the northern block with a beastly pack chasing after them. Seconds later, they heard a thunderous bang that shook the entire building. It was accompanied by anguished shrieks of monsters and angry bellows of the abomination. Meanwhile, they continued fleeing across a large corridor soaked with crimson illumination falling through its expansive windows.

Daley looked over his shoulder to see a large group of the three-headed freaks, who had managed to avoid the blast, still running after them. Then suddenly, he heard a loud crack and turned back to the grisly sight of five horned demons crawling through a shattered window. The beasts rushed forward, downing two soldiers, ripping open one's chest while slitting the other one's throat.

Daley grabbed his pistol and fired three times, taking out one of the creatures by shattering its skull. The remaining eight soldiers also started firing, killing three more demons, which allowed them to reach the back exit, leaving the corpses of two of their fallen comrades behind.

After they burst through the door, Daley turned and threw another grenade at the monsters pursuing them before joining his men as they rushed through the empty streets laden with human corpses. He saw numerous cracks in the inner city wall, allowing the thick white mist to seep inside. With gunfire and muffled screams coming from all directions, they retreated to the side of one of the taverns. There they finally stopped, panting, looking warily at the murky streets.

Daley gritted his teeth, trying to ignore the aching wound in his belly he had suffered during their initial expedition with Kyron. Meanwhile, one of the soldiers, a young black-haired man with brown eyes, stepped forward. "What now, Sir?" he asked in a trembling voice.

Daley looked around, trying desperately to devise a viable course of action. However, nothing in his long years of service could've prepared him for the situation they were currently in. Seeing hopelessness on the Major's face, the black-haired soldier's eyes trembled, and he covered them with his hands before releasing an anguished gasp.

"We must remain calm," Daley uttered. "We must rally with our remaining forces and take back the city."

"What if everyone is already dead?" a soldier with a green bandanna tied around his long blonde hair asked, then chuckled nervously, sparks of lunacy glinting in his eyes.

Daley was opening his mouth to answer when he was interrupted by eerie howls coming from every direction. Seconds later, hairy wolflike beasts started crawling from the mist, gnashing their fangs while leering ravenously at the squad with bulging yellow eyes. Without waiting for Daley's orders, the soldier with the bandanna opened fire, and the rest of the squad soon joined him.

The beasts scattered, nimbly avoiding the shots while barking and growling excitedly before charging forward. Several wolfmen fell, but the remaining ones reached the squad and started picking them apart.

While backing away, brandishing the combat knife in one hand while firing the pistol with the other, Daley saw his troops falling one by one, their bodies ripped to pieces while they screamed in pain and terror. Not before long, he was the only one left, his back pressed against the wall, surrounded by monsters, their barks mocking his futile struggle.

With his heart pounding, Daley turned, then rushed along the wall, dodging beastly swipes before turning the corner and continuing until he reached the tavern entrance. He kicked the door open and leaped inside, almost slipping on the thick layer of blood and gore covering the floor.

There were at least twenty bodies splattered across the main area, with the bartender lying on the counter, his jaw missing, and his dead eyes staring blankly at the ceiling. Not having time to fully take in the horrific sight, Daley gritted his teeth, shut the door behind him, then ran across the room into a narrow corridor that led him to the back exit.

Without looking over his shoulder, Daley leaped back into the street and continued sprinting, breathing heavily, the wound in his belly throbbing, sending jolts of pain every step he took. Howls were coming from all around, but as he continued rushing across narrow alleyways, they became more distant as the beasts moved on in search of easier prey.

Daley stopped, leaning against a tall building, then looked down to see the blood seeping through the bandages on his waist. He coughed hoarsely a few times, then looked around, his gaze settling on the spires of the Royal Palace and the demonic figures soaring around them. In his mind, the grimmest of thoughts were rising, and he tried desperately to push away the madness so he could continue carrying out his duties to the Intercontinental Military Force.

The city has fallen. The communication channels were severed. With no way to rally my troops, my only objective is to ensure the safety of Kyron. There may still be military trucks left by the palace; if that's the case, I could use them to escape the Capital.

With his mission now clear, Daley felt the clutches of panic loosening, allowing him to regain control. He took a deep breath, then with one hand pressed to his belly, started quickly creeping toward the palace.

The sounds of fighting now had ceased, and the eerie silence of the inner city was disturbed only by an occasional howl. Shortly, the Major reached the main gates leading into the palace grounds. They were hanging wide open with several military trucks standing in front. One had its tires blown and windows shattered. Thankfully, the other seemed mostly intact, and Daley figured he might use it to escape the Capital.

After having a quick look around, the Major entered and continued rushing through the paved pathway, crossing an expansive meadow. Shortly, he reached a set of steps leading to a large entrance door, standing ajar with a single corpse of one of the Kyron's bodyguards wearing a dark-blue suit lying in front. Daley knelt down and examined the body to see that the man's neck was crushed with his eyes bulging out of their sockets in an expression of utmost terror. The Major took the pistol he found beside the deceased guard, shoved it under his belt, then carefully stepped over the corpse and peeked inside.

There were more blue-suited corpses in the expansive corridors of the palace, its carpeted floors splattered with a heavy layer of blood. As Daley slowly walked forward, he observed that most guards seemed to be choked to death, just like the one by the entrance. Although, there were a few with their chests torn open or their insides ripped from their belly.

As he moved closer to the royal chambers, the number of corpses kept increasing, and terror started creeping into Daley's mind, urging him to abandon his orders and look out for himself. He stopped a corridor away from the entrance to the royal hall and looked around, hesitating.

It seems unlikely that with the injuries Kyron already suffered, he could've escaped whatever evil force caused all this mayhem. Perhaps I should try to get out while there's still a chance. If the wolfmen tracked me down, I don't know whether I'd have enough strength to escape them again.

Daley turned and was about to go back when he saw Kyron standing in the middle of the corridor.

"Hello, Major," the man spoke. "It's nice of you to return to me while the others have fled with their tails between their legs." The ruler of Orox smiled faintly, then walked past confused Daley, crossed the corridor, stopped just by the door, and uttered: "You're coming?" before entering the royal hall.

Major glanced at the corpses lying on the floor, his mind racing, trying to explain what was happening.

Did Kyron lose his mind? And how is he walking around with his injuries? I didn't see him carrying any weapons, so I may be able to subdue and drag him out of here if things turn ugly. Still, I should try to convince him to leave with me since I can't afford to cause a commotion with demons soaring above us.

Clutching his pistol, Daley walked into the expansive hall to find Kyron sitting on his throne, his penetrating brown eyes peering vacantly before him. The Major approached, stopping about ten yards away, then spoke: "Sir, we need to get out of here. The city has fallen, and I can't get in contact with any of my men."

Kyron didn't answer, continuing to stare blankly in front of him.

Daley gritted his teeth, then took a few more steps forward. "Sir, what happened here?"

"It's almost time," the ruler of Orox uttered hoarsely.

"Time for what? What in god's name are you talking about?"

Kyron smirked, finally fixing his eyes on Daley. "Time for me to embrace the power given to me by the gods and liberate our land from the ghoulish presence."

"We need to get out of here now," Daley insisted, then approached the throne and grabbed Kyron by the arm. "Come with me, Sir. We need to retreat to Talos and rally humanity's remaining troops."

"Retreat?" Kyron cackled. "I've never fled from any foe, and I'm not about to start now. I'll defeat this evil, and you, Daley, will help me."

The Major sighed, then looked over his shoulder, listening, feeling increasingly anxious and irritated. "Fine," he uttered. "We'll defeat the evil. But first, you need to come with me. We don't have time for—"

Daley felt something slimy wrap around his wrist, and he turned to see a scaly tentacle coming out of Kyron's mouth. The Major gasped and stepped back, trying to yank his arm out, but the ghastly limb tightened its grip, preventing his escape.

Daley bellowed, then grabbed the knife from his waist and sank its blade into the quivering flesh, drawing blood and forcing it to let go. Finally free, the Major continued backing away, holding the knife in one hand and his pistol in the other, his finger on the trigger trembling. "Who are you!?" Daley screamed. "What have you done to Kyron?"

The bleeding tentacle retracted into the man's mouth. He smiled broadly, stood up from the throne, and started walking toward Daley. "You'll be the first to join me in the holy union, Major," Kyron said. "Only with our flesh and blood mended into a single entity can we defeat the cosmic horror that invaded our world."

"This is madness!" Daley screamed, feeling like he was on the brink of lunacy. "Am I to believe that you, Kyron, willingly merged with some demonic entity in a promise of a greater power?"

"This is the only way," Kyron said firmly, extending his hands toward the Major. "Do not resist, friend. I only want what's best for this world and my people. That's the only thing that I've always wanted."

Daley shook his head in bafflement and was about to turn, intending to flee, when Kyron's hands exploded, giving way to over a dozen tentacles that sprang forward and wrapped around Daley from head to toe.

The Major bellowed in horror and started frantically pressing the trigger, but most of his shots missed, and the ones that hit the writhing limbs didn't seem to do much harm.

"This is the only way," Kyron gargled hoarsely, his voice now barely human, permeated with creepy clicks and screeches.

As Daley continued squirming, Kyron's chest burst open, and out of it, thin tendrils shot toward the Major, piercing through his skin and burrowing deep into his flesh. Then, he felt his essence being drained as his consciousness quickly faded, absorbed by Kyron's demonic form.

Keri

Keri opened her eyes, then wobbled, almost tumbling to the ground. It felt like she had awoken from a long dream, but she couldn't quite recall what it was about. She looked around, realizing she was standing beside a wide road with the tall buildings of Atheta looming in the distance, soaked in the evening twilight. Her hands still grasped the giant sword covered in the putrid liquid that shot from the hag's heart.

Suddenly, Keri heard a distant rumbling and turned to see a large truck moving toward her. It stopped about five yards away, and its doors opened. Inside, she saw her old crew – Glenn, William, Tobias, and Anika, who was sitting in the driver's seat.

"Well, what are you waiting for?" William asked, smirking while twirling his revolver. "Hop in, girly. We have a job to do."

Keri's eyes trembled, her bafflement quickly turning to sorrow. She hesitated, then got inside the truck and sat down, putting the greatsword on her lap.

"That's a nice weapon you have right there, darling," William said, smiling from ear to ear.

Keri looked into his eyes, then lowered her gaze while biting her lower lip. "I'm sorry I couldn't save you guys," she mumbled.

For a bit, they sat in silence. Then, Anika turned the key in the ignition and pressed on the gas. After the truck started moving, she glanced over her shoulder before saying: "It's okay, Keri. We don't blame you."

"That's right," Tobias concurred, placing his hand on Keri's shoulder. "I'm happy we get to go on one last mission together."

Keri's heart trembled, and she sighed deeply before raising her eyes again. "But… where exactly are we?"

"In our own personal hell," William said, then cackled cheerfully.

"Oh shut up, you," Anika muttered, her eyes fixed on the road. "If it was up to you, we'd never leave this place. You *love* shooting those freaks."

William cackled again. "Guilty as charged!"

"Glenn, could you explain?" Anika said irritably.

The burly bearded man nodded and fixed his eyes on Keri before speaking: "We woke up in the outskirts some weeks ago, maybe months – it's hard to tell in this place. We were told we need to slay the entity in the city center to get out of here, and that's what we've been trying to do all that time."

"Told by whom?" Keri asked.

Glenn shrugged. "None of us can remember. Anyway, the point is that we've been failing miserably, getting killed every day, no matter the tactics we tried. And each day, we awaken in the outskirts to repeat our futile struggle."

"But now that you're here, everything will be different," Tobias said, smiling broadly. "Our whole crew – finally back together."

Keri bit her lower lip, looking at the tall city buildings and the beastly figures shambling in the slums. "Do you guys… remember everything that happened?"

"Not a damn thing!" William exclaimed happily.

"I remember," Glenn uttered, then lowered his eyes. "But I would rather not talk about it."

"How about you, Keri?" Tobias asked, looking at her intently. "Do you remember how you got here?"

Keri didn't answer, her eyes fixed on the dark silhouettes in the distance, her heart pounding in anticipation of another battle. For the time being, she decided to abandon her speculations about what was happening and focus on solving the problems at hand.

"They're already coming for us!" Anika exclaimed, then pressed on the brakes.

The crew exited the truck and started arming themselves with pistols, shotguns, rifles, and grenades stacked in the trunk.

"I believe this belongs to you," Tobias said, extending Keri a revolver with a large barrel.

She looked at it briefly, then smiled faintly and shook her head. "This belonged to the old me. The one who was weak and cowardly and brought all this mess upon you. But I'm not afraid anymore. I'll get us out of here no matter what."

"That's the spirit!" William exclaimed while tying the third grenade belt around his waist.

From a distance came dozens of ferocious howls and ghoulish gargles. Keri stepped forward to see a horde of no less than a hundred wolfmen and fishmen rushing at them from the slums. "Are these the former citizens of Atheta?" she asked, looking at Glenn, who stood with a large shotgun in his hands.

"I wouldn't worry about that," the man said. "Just like the rest of us, they rise after every battle. They are also trapped by this curse, and I'm sure they welcome even the momentary respite."

"What's the matter, Keri?" Tobias asked, stepping toward them.

She pondered briefly, then shook her head. "Never mind," she said, then grasped the handle of her greatsword and rushed forward to meet the approaching abominations.

74

Keri heard William's excited scream, and soon, bullets started flying, taking down several beasts running in front. She told herself this was just some otherworldly realm, and she wasn't about to engage in another merciless slaughter of the innocents. Still, Keri hesitated slightly before the engagement, almost allowing one of the wolfmen to sink its fangs into her flesh. However, she put her doubts away at the last moment and embraced the battle frenzy rising within.

Keri started tearing through the monstrous army with mighty swings, eviscerating at least four beasts with each attack. Several creatures slipped past her and began rushing toward the crew, but they were immediately downed by a barrage of bullets.

Keri made quick work of the wolfmen, then moved to the fishmen running in the back, gargling angrily. Some of them were carrying large spears, which they started throwing, trying to impale her, but she dodged all of their attacks gracefully while continuing to hack and slash, lifting blood and gore into the air, which drenched her from head to toe.

"Not bad at all!" William exclaimed after the last fishman fell. "If we continue at this pace, we might actually have a chance." He quickly approached, then clapped her on the back, smiling ear to ear. "Just be careful now. The ghouls in the city have guns."

Keri widened her eyes. "Guns?" Just as the word left her mouth, a bullet flew above her head. She turned to see a bizarre creature with charred skin and burning red eyes standing by a ramshackle lodge, holding a rifle.

William raised his revolvers and started firing, downing the monster before it could take another shot. The man then turned to Keri and gave her a broad smile. "They're not very accurate, but there are hordes of them scattered across the city. I think I even saw one carrying a grenade launcher, so watch out."

Keri peered at the man's smiling face. "Are you seriously enjoying this?"

Something flashed briefly in William's eyes. He glanced over his shoulder at Anika, Tobias, and Glenn walking toward them. Then, he leaned closer and whispered into Keri's ear: "Someone needs to keep the morale up." He then withdrew and hollered: "Come on now! Let's send those freaks back to hell!"

Quickly, they started moving through the slums. Looking warily at crooked buildings and makeshift huts, Keri recalled the numerous missions she went on with her crew. They would question the locals, arrest the suspects, and sometimes even get into shootouts with the criminal drug dealers. Then, after a long day, they would return to the station, shower, and unwind in one of the local bars, chatting, joking, and drinking away their troubles. She also remembered her growing discontent caused by the futility of their battle, which eventually led to her removing herself from such nightly outings, taking a leave of absence, and traveling to Exter.

At this moment, Keri would've given anything to return to such simpler times; when she only needed to worry about corrupt human nature and knew nothing about the eldritch beasts wandering the dark corners of the world. "I'm sorry, guys," she uttered, feeling her eyes tremble. "I should never have distanced myself."

"I never held any ill will against you," Anika said.

"None of us did," Tobias agreed. "We knew that eventually, you'd return to us."

Keri smiled faintly, trying her hardest to push away the tears.

"This is all very lovely, but this is hardly the place or time to exchange such pleasantries," William said, smirking. "We're about to enter a real meat grinder, so you better get yourselves ready."

"You're one to talk," Anika uttered. "Like those monsters haven't already been alerted by your excessive hollering."

William cackled, then fixed his gaze on the tall apartment buildings looming in the distance. "It seems that the welcoming party is already here," he said, pointing at the group of ghouls gathering just by the rusty sign proclaiming "Atheta" in big white letters with the words "Leave your dreams behind" graffitied just below the city name. Many creatures were armed with pistols and rifles and wore bullet-proof vests.

The crew took cover behind a wreckage of an old truck, observing more and more of the zombified troops shambling the streets and taking positions in high-rise buildings, seemingly controlled by some invisible force.

"Can you reach them from here?" William asked, looking at Anika.

The woman nodded, then grabbed her rifle, aimed, and fired at the sniper on the balcony of the closest apartment building. They saw the ghoul wobble, topple over the railing and fall to the ground. Seconds later, a cacophony of moans broke throughout the enemy ranks as they started moving out of the city and shambling toward the crew. Anika, joined by Tobias, continued shooting, trying to take down the snipers while the others prepared to meet the upcoming force.

"There seems to be even more of them this time," William muttered, peeking from behind the corner of their cover.

"Will our usual plan still work?" Tobias asked while reloading his rifle.

"Yeah," William said. "You just focus on taking down those snipers."

"So, what's the plan?" Keri asked, looking around anxiously.

"No time to explain, girly," William said. "You just stay put before we clean out the front attackers – we'll need your abilities once we get into the city."

"All done!" Anika exclaimed, shifting her attention from the tall buildings to the approaching horde, now just a hundred yards away.

William and Glenn glanced at each other, then left the cover and started sprinting to opposite sides. The bullets began flying their way, but they dodged them nimbly while taking cover behind the ramshackle houses and broken-down cars. Keri watched as the two men reached the back of the enemy formation, then started throwing grenades while Tobias and Anika continued shooting at the ghouls shambling in front.

Soon, everything was engulfed by numerous thunderous blasts that lifted the monsters high into the air, dismembering their bodies and ripping their flesh. The mayhem lasted for several minutes until no ghouls were left moving, and the area before them was turned into a charred field laden with mutilated corpses.

"All clear!" William shouted while coming out of the cover.

The rest of the crew soon approached his position. Keri widened her eyes after noticing several bleeding bullet holes on William's left arm.

"Don't mind these," the man said after catching her gaze. "This is actually better than we usually do."

"Have you ever reached the center?"

"Just about," William mumbled. "We usually get stopped by giants in the inner city."

"Giants?" Keri raised her eyebrows.

"You'll see." William smiled. "Our weapons don't do them much harm, but your sword may prove perfect for the job. In fact—"

"Take cover!" Glenn screamed, yanking Keri and Anika backward. Moments later, a massive explosion launched everyone into the air.

Keri's vision darkened momentarily as she was flung across the field before slamming heavily into the wall of a wooden lodge. After regaining her senses, she saw Glenn and Anika on the ground beside her. Meanwhile, Tobias lay by the truck that recently served them as a cover, and William was sprawled on the opposite side of the field.

"Grenade launcher on top of the western block!" they heard Tobias yell as he got up and started firing his rifle.

Cursing, Anika grabbed her gun and also began blasting, soon taking down a ghoulish soldier before he could take another shot. Then, everyone hurried to William to find the man unconscious, lying in a pool of blood spurting from a massive wound in his abdomen.

"He's done for," Glenn said grimly, then raised his eyes to the rest of the crew. "I'm sorry. I should've warned you sooner, but my senses don't seem to work as well as they used to."

"Can't do anything about it now," Anika uttered, peering at her fallen comrade, her eyes trembling slightly. "Damn, I'll never get used to seeing him like this."

"We better get inside the city before more of them show up," Tobias said. "Glenn, could you fetch the grenade launcher? Hopefully, we can use it against the giants."

Glenn nodded, then hurried toward the large apartment block while Tobias, Keri, and Anika stepped into the city and hid in one of the narrow alleyways. As they lingered, shrouded by shadows, they heard the ghouls shambling past them.

"If we try to lure them out, more just keep coming until we get overwhelmed," Tobias whispered. "We tried many tactics, but making an initial push and sneaking toward the city center always worked best. Still, we were never able to get past the giants."

Keri pressed her lips tightly, wondering what kind of monstrosities she was about to face. "How many times exactly did you try this?"

"Too many to bother counting," Anika mumbled bitterly. "At first, we couldn't even get past the slum dwellers. We improved greatly over time but hit the wall with those overgrown beasts. They always notice us as soon as we get close. I think they can pick up our scent."

They heard footsteps and turned to see Glenn ambling toward them with a grenade launcher hanging over his shoulder.

"All right, let's go," Tobias whispered, then started creeping forward.

Through the dark alleys and desolate streets, they moved toward the city center. There were groups of armed ghouls wandering about, but they successfully sneaked past by staying in the shadows, away from the lampposts and the faint lights coming from the windows. Then, as the sky above turned from gray to black, dozens of massive humps emerged in the distance, shambling in the large square.

After getting a bit closer, Keri realized that those were the giants her crew mentioned, standing at least thirty feet tall, their bodies made from red pulsating flesh. They had thick legs, long arms, and a round head with bulging pitch-black eyes leering from the middle of their ghastly face, just above a large nose and wide mouth, twisted into an uncanny grin exposing large rectangular teeth.

"This is it," Anika whispered, looking at the abominations shambling in the distance. "A few more steps, and they'll notice us." She turned toward the rest of the crew. "You're ready?"

"Let's do this," Keri said, gripping her greatsword, trying to invoke the same energy she felt pulsating through her while battling the hags.

"Alright, Glenn, start," Anika said.

The man nodded, then grabbed the grenade launcher from his shoulder, aimed it at the closest giant, and pressed the trigger. Seconds later, the monster's torso exploded, splattering black blood on the ground and making the creature crumble to its knees, bellowing in pain. At the same time, all the remaining giants turned their heads toward the crew and, screaming madly, started charging, the ground shaking under their massive feet.

Glenn fired one more time from the grenade launcher, downing another abomination by exploding part of its face. Meanwhile, Tobias and Anika grabbed their rifles and started shooting, aiming for the monsters' eyes.

Seeing the giants approaching, Keri took a deep breath, feeling her eyes lighting up with the emerald gleam. Then, after releasing a fierce scream, she rushed forward to meet the abominations head-on.

The closest giant opened its maw widely, then got on all fours and jumped forward, intending to swallow Keri whole. But, with the swing of her sword, she split its head into two before dodging aside to avoid its massive frame that dropped to the ground and slid on the pavement before finally stopping and going limp.

The remaining giants bellowed angrily and rushed toward Keri, extending their arms and trying to grab her. However, she dodged their swipes nimbly while hacking and slashing, downing the creatures one by one, drenching the ground with their pungent insides.

The more monsters she took down, the more vigorous her blows became, and the brighter the emerald light gleamed from her eyes. After dodging the stomp of one particularly large giant, Keri cackled excitedly, a broad grin distorting her face. She then stepped forward, with a single swipe cutting off the monster's legs before jumping on top of it and stabbing its chest repeatedly as it bellowed in pain and anger before finally succumbing to its injuries.

The entire battle only lasted several minutes. After the last giant fell, Keri turned around, breathing heavily, looking at her crew standing in the cover of a tall apartment building. After they approached, Keri saw a fearful awe gleaming in their eyes, making her wonder whether they saw her as human or one of the beasts – a vessel to the forbidden energy of the primordial void.

"We should keep moving," Tobias said with a noticeable tremble in his voice. "The rest of the ghouls will soon be here. We need to reach the city center before they show up."

Keri nodded, wiped off the giants' black blood from her face, turned, and started ambling toward the tall buildings. After reaching the edge of the square, she glanced over her shoulder to see Anika, Glenn, and Tobias following about ten yards behind. After catching her gaze, Glenn and Anika lowered their heads, and even Tobias turned away, seemingly afraid to peer into the emerald light gleaming from Keri's eyes.

She turned back to the building, then sighed, her initial elation of seeing her old crew now replaced by grim ponderations about the trials she was made to face.

Is it all just some form of mockery devised by the Greater Will to show me that I'm no better than the monsters I fight? That I, despite knowing that most of them are just anguished spirits turned against their will, have no problem in slaughtering them indiscriminately? At this point, am I really trying to save anyone, or am I just wallowing in my gratuitous rage and self-righteousness?

With such gloomy thoughts, Keri ambled through the empty streets, the blade of the greatsword resting on her shoulder. After the last few battles, it started to feel like the ancient weapon was becoming an extension of her limbs, and Keri feared that this was a part of some bizarre transformation that may morph her into something inhuman.

The tall commercial buildings parted before her to reveal a town center consisting of a wide round field of black obsidian rock. In its middle stood a grotesque altar made from dark demonic skulls. Kneeling before it was the Queen of Filth with her hands clasped and her long hair and black gown fluttering in the wind.

After Keri stepped into the field, the woman rose from the ground, turned toward her, then smirked out of her pale visage framing her abyssal gaze. "So I see you finally made it to my eternal playgrounds."

"Why are you here?" Keri asked. "Why don't you let the citizens of Atheta rest in peace? Was taking their lives not enough to fulfill your twisted ambition? Why do you linger here instead of returning to the shadow, demon?"

"These spirits were given to me by the Greater God," the Queen snarled. "I can keep them in this domain as long as I please. And I intend to do so until I deplete them of their shining and they are ready to be absorbed by the primordial void."

"So, you really feel justified in causing all this anguish?"

"I have no intention of discussing my aspirations with such pesky little vermin as you, Struggler. So you can either get out of my way or succumb to my will, just like all those precious people you're trying so hard to protect."

Keri took a step forward, raising her sword. "I've defeated you once; I can do it again," she said firmly.

The Queen chuckled. "If you defeated me, why I'm still here?"

Suddenly, Keri heard Tobias shouting, "The monsters are coming!" and turned to see dark silhouettes approaching from afar. Then, she fixed her eyes on the Queen again before gripping the handle of her greatsword and charging forward, her emerald eyes gleaming brighter than ever before.

Even if I become a demon myself by the end of this journey, it will be worth it if I can save at least a few of these unfortunate spirits from the tortures of the damned.

Keri screamed and leaped forward, swinging her sword, intending to cut the Queen in half. However, the woman shifted out of the way at the last moment, leaving black streaks in the air. She then raised her arms, her fingers turning into tentacles that wrapped around the Struggler, constricting her movements.

Keri leaned over, trying to sink her teeth into one of the quivering limbs, but the Queen immediately withdrew. Then, she waved her hands, summoning an obsidian spear that she threw at Keri, piercing her shoulder and making her tumble. Moments later, the Queen waved her hands again, conjuring a thin spike that shot from under the ground, and Keri barely slid out of the way before it could impale her torso.

"You have no power here, Struggler!" the Queen exclaimed. "Kneel before me, or I'll tear your spirit to shreds!"

Keri heard the shots on the other side of the square, and she turned to see her crew firing at the horde of ghouls, wolfmen, and fishmen, charging at them at full speed. Gritting her teeth, she grabbed the spear and pulled it out of her shoulder, splattering blood on the obsidian surface. She then got up, looking contemptuously into the Queen's dark eyes.

"Ready to give up? Or do you want to play a bit longer?" the demon mocked, smiling from ear to ear, revealing her sharp fangs.

Keri grunted, then leaped forward again, biting her lower lip, trying to reach for the power residing within.

"You're so tiresome," the Queen grumbled, then summoned another spear and threw it at Keri. However, this time, she dodged out of the way before leaping forward and swinging at the Queen.

The demon shifted again, leaving behind a dark streak. Keri followed her, swinging ferociously, but the Queen clicked her fingers, which caused her body to melt into the ground before reappearing about twenty yards away. Then, she opened her mouth and out of it unleashed a swarm of black flies, which surrounded Keri, blocking her vision. Seconds later, she felt another spear piercing her back, barely missing her heart.

Keri wobbled, feeling the taste of blood in her mouth. Through the insect swarm, she saw her crewmates backing away as the monsters began to pour into the square. Meanwhile, the Queen started cackling madly, her sharp voice echoing ghostly in the night.

Keri gasped a few times, then released a ferocious scream. The gleam from her eyes engulfed everything around, and for a moment, only she and the Queen existed, floating in the emerald void.

Keri leaped forward and extended her hand, grabbing the demon's bare shoulders. As she peered into the abyss looming behind the Queen's eyes, she caught a flash of fright and uncertainty. Then, she leaned forward and sank her teeth into the Queen's neck before the demon could shift out of the way again.

A loud shriek pierced through the cosmos, and Keri saw the lands far away inhabited by creatures vaguely resembling humans. She also saw the Chamber of Blood with the ghastly woman standing among the sea of gore, peering at Keri with a broad grin on her face. Then followed a vast expansion of darkness filled with images of places and people that were changing rapidly, as if she was soaring through the memories of the being who existed for thousands of years.

Finally, the void parted, and they returned to the obsidian field, Keri's teeth still biting the Queen's neck. The demon groaned, then pushed her away before shifting aside and swiping at the air with her sharp nails, opening the gap in space. She gave Keri another contemptuous glare before stepping through and vanishing out of sight.

Abruptly, the scenery changed. The town vanished, giving way to a plain desert of purple sand with multicolored stars gleaming in the vast sky above. Keri's entire crew: William, Glenn, Anika, and Tobias, stood about twenty yards away with a large group of people behind them. Most of them seemed disoriented, looking around with wide eyes. However, a few gazed at Keri, smiling faintly from their ashen faces.

"Thanks for one last operation, girly!" William exclaimed, giving her a wink.

Keri noticed a slight tremble in Tobias's eyes as the man stepped forward and opened his mouth, intending to speak. But unfortunately, everything faded into the thick mist before he could utter a single word.

Sofia

At some point, despite the dread pulsating through her veins and the wolfmen howling outside, Sofia drifted into an uneasy slumber. She wandered through the dark streets, hearing beasts scamper somewhere nearby, trying to prevent the sob from leaving her mouth so as not to alert the demons to her location. The roads kept branching, outstretching along the tall apartment buildings with shattered windows, leering at her like the eyes of some gargantuan beast. The darkness around her was only dispersed by a few lampposts, flashing eerily, their ghostly illumination only adding to Sofia's agitated state.

Suddenly, she saw someone standing in the shadowy alley. Sofia gasped and was about to run when the person stepped into the open, revealing their sunken visage framed by brown hair tied into a single plait.

"Anabel?" Sofia uttered fearfully. "What are you doing here?"

Her sister started walking toward her, her long dark-blue dress fluttering in the faint breeze. She stopped several yards away, looking at Sofia with a sorrowful expression before speaking in a tired, hoarse voice: "Why do you keep running, little one? Why did you refuse to follow me into the land of flourish?"

"I-I was afraid," Sofia whimpered. "Last time I saw you, you turned into…"

Ghastly images arose in her mind of Anabel's face transforming into the visage of a grotesque beast, and she took a step back, fearing that the same might happen again.

"You don't need to be afraid," Anabel said. "It was never my intention to hurt you, and it kills me to see you like this. You should just let go and follow me. Everyone is waiting for you."

"Everyone?" Sofia turned her head to see more figures standing in the alley, their faces shrouded by darkness.

"Eric, Adam, Alfred, and all the residents of Lerwick – everyone's already here. Little sis, you should take Julie with you and come to us, so we could be one big family again."

"How would I do that?"

"Take this," Anabel said, extending her an intricate knife with a silver handle and a black curved blade etched with a series of twisting serpentine lines, glistening in the twilight.

A shiver ran down Sofia's spine, and her body trembled. "I don't know if I can do it," she whimpered.

"You can, sweetie," Anabel said, then stepped closer and placed the knife on Sofia's palm before adding: "We all believe in you."

Sofia shuddered and opened her eyes. She stared blankly at the yellow wall for some time, breathing heavily, feeling the slightest relief after realizing it was all a dream before remembering that her reality wasn't much better than the most grievous of nightmares.

She turned her head to see Julie drowsing on the bed, holding onto her injured arm. Meanwhile, Faye was standing by the closet, trying to peek out the window through the small gap.

"Are they still out there?" Sofia asked.

Faye glanced at her, then fixed her eyes on the window again. "I'm not sure. But I haven't heard anything for a while."

Sofia was about to get up from the floor when she felt something cold in her palm. She lowered her gaze to see her hand grasping the silver handle of the curved knife. Her eyes widened, and a gasp escaped her mouth as her mind quivered, trying to comprehend the implications of her dreams spilling into the waking world.

"Is something the matter?" Faye asked, taking a step toward her.

Sofia quickly hid the dagger under her shirt, then turned and smiled lightly. "Nothing. I'm sorry. I thought I saw a spider."

Faye raised her eyebrows. "A spider, really? That's what you're worried about right now?"

Sofia shrugged apologetically. Faye looked at her for a bit longer, then stepped to the bed and knelt beside Julie, looking into the woman's drowsy eyes. "Hey. How are you holding up?"

"I'm fine," Julie muttered, then coughed a few times, and Sofia noticed a tiny stream of yellow drool seeping from her mouth.

Suddenly, the beastly scream engulfed everything, making the women shudder. They lingered until the horrible voice completely faded away. Then, Faye stood up, giving both sisters an intent look. "Should we try going out?"

Sofia trembled at the thought of facing the wolfmen again, remembering their ravenous bulging eyes and sharp fangs. "Perhaps we should wait a bit longer?" she suggested.

Julie coughed again while wheezing heavily and nursing her injured arm.

"We can't just stay in this room forever," Faye said. "Your sister needs medical attention. If we keep delaying, she might not survive the trip over the sea."

"I said I'm fine," Julie uttered, then started scratching the back of her neck.

Faye sighed, then stepped to the closet covering the window. "Sofia, help me move this."

84

Hesitantly, Sofia got up and, together with Faye, pushed the closet out of the way. Then, they both peered outside at the desolate streets drenched with the crimson illumination of the moon. After a little while, Faye stepped from the window and sighed deeply before speaking: "Well, I don't know about you, girls, but I'm heading out. I'll go crazy if I stay inside this room any longer."

Julie snickered, then got out of bed, smirking. "You and me both," she said, this time with much more vigor.

"Are you sure?" Sofia asked, looking at her sister intently.

Julie nodded, then, with surprising ease, pushed the bed from the door.

"Does your hand not hurt anymore?" Faye asked.

"Not really. I suddenly feel a lot better."

The three lingered for several uneasy seconds. Then, Faye nodded, stepped to the door, and carefully opened it, producing an eerie creak. The three peered into the hallway laden with bits of broken furniture. The front door was wide open, and the shelf they used to barricade it lay on the floor. Sofia also noticed blood splattered on the wood from when Julie stabbed the wolfman trying to get in.

They shared glances with one another, then started carefully advancing before stepping into the desolate street, where they were immediately enveloped by a cold wind. Shivering, they began creeping forward, the sisters grasping the obsidian-bladed swords while Faye clutched her shotgun. Julie walked slightly in front of Sofia, scratching the back of her neck, which was now bright red.

"Are you really okay?" Sofia whispered.

"I said I am!" Julie snarled, giving her an angry look.

"Hey, stay quiet, you two," Faye muttered.

"Oh, just shut up," Julie said, locking her glinty eyes on the woman. "I'm sick of you ordering us around."

Faye blinked several times, then frowned. "Well, if you don't like it, you two can just go on your own. I already said it multiple times."

"Give us the shotgun then," Julie uttered, taking a step toward Faye, who, in turn, took a step back.

"Easy now. I really don't want to shoot you, but I will if you continue acting like this."

Julie snickered contemptuously.

"Let's just all calm down," Sofia said, her voice trembling. "There's no need to fight with each other. We—"

She stopped mid-sentence after noticing a shadowy silhouette in the dark alley several dozen yards away. Moments later, a cold gust of wind enveloped her, carrying a ghostly whisper: "Do it, Sofia." She gasped a few times, then took a step back, feeling the dagger under her shirt pressing into her skin.

"What's wrong?" Faye mumbled, looking around nervously.

Sofia glanced at her, then peered at the alley again, but the silhouette wasn't there anymore. "Did you hear it?"

"Hear what?" Faye asked, continuing to look around.

"I heard it," Julie said, then stepped closer, leaned over, and whispered into Sofia's ear: "We can take her if we both rush her at once. She's just bluffing – she won't actually shoot us."

"What are you two whispering about?" Faye uttered, fear radiating from her voice.

"Now!" Julie screamed, her eyes gleaming with yellow light, then turned and lunged forward.

The shotgun blast pierced through the eerie tranquility. With horror, Sofia watched her sister collapse, blood spurting from numerous wounds in her chest. Then, her eyes shifted to the gun in Faye's hands, smoke rising from its barrel.

"What did you do!" Sofia screamed, feeling the blind rage building inside, pushing away her innate timidness.

"Don't move!" Faye yelled, then started backing away. "I'm going on my own! I'm… sorry for this."

Another gust of wind came seemingly out of nowhere, fluttering Sofia's hair and whispering into her ear, urging her to charge the woman in front. She turned slightly to see Anabel, Eric, and Adam standing in the alley, smiling broadly. Then, gripping the handle of her obsidian sword, she took a step forward.

"No!" Faye screamed. "Don't make me do this!"

The anger painted Sofia's thoughts bright red. She bellowed, then raised her sword and charged forward. Faye shrieked, then turned the shotgun toward her and pushed the trigger, but nothing happened. Moments later, Sofia got close and started swinging wildly, intending to cut the woman who killed her sister into pieces. Faye dodged two attacks, then lunged forward, bashing Sofia's head with the butt of the gun.

The world grew dark, and she felt the sword slipping out of her hands. Then followed another blow, bringing Sofia to the ground. Gasping, she tilted her head and, through the humming mist, saw Faye turning away, intending to flee.

"DO IT! DO IT! DO IT!" Anabel screamed in her head.

Gritting her teeth, Sofia grabbed the knife hidden under her shirt and sank it into the back of Faye's leg. The woman shrieked in pain and tumbled to the ground. Heaving, feeling blood leaking from her forehead,

Sofia crawled on top of her, then grasped Faye's neck while the voice in her head continued screaming, "DO IT," becoming distorted and less human with every repetition.

They struggled for several seconds until Faye pushed Sofia off with her healthy leg. She then grabbed the knife still lodged into her flesh and pulled it out while screaming in pain before turning the weapon toward Sofia. "Stop it!" Faye screamed. "Just snap out of it!"

The fear was beginning to creep back into her mind, giving rise to doubt. Sofia tilted her head to see the entire population of Lerwick in the middle of the street, with Anabel, Eric, and Adam standing in front, smiling broadly, their eyes radiating a purple gleam. "Do it, Sofia! Do it!" they spoke in unison.

She turned her head to the sword lying on the ground. Then, she took a deep breath and grabbed it before lunging at Faye, who was screaming something Sofia could no longer understand.

She raised her sword before bringing it down, aiming for Faye's head, but the woman rolled out of the way before lodging the knife into Sofia's chest. She felt blood filling her mouth, then wobbled before dropping to the ground. She tried to move, but her strength was quickly fading, along with her vision.

Sofia tilted her head, wanting to look at the faces of her family one last time. But instead, she saw a horde of demons standing amidst an obsidian plane, grinning broadly, the echo of their mocking cackles rising to the purple skies above. Then, their voices also started to fade, giving way to the silence of the void.

Darren

"They haven't moved in a while. Maybe they're asleep," Darren whispered, looking at the winged demons perched on the spires of the Royal Palace. He turned to Christa and Nina standing behind him in the narrow alley. "I think we should go for it."

"Perhaps we should wait just a little bit longer?" Christa suggested.

"There's no time," Nina whimpered, her pleading blue eyes fixed on Darren. "We need to get to Keri. Otherwise, it will all be over."

The man looked at the little girl, then shifted his gaze back to Christa. The woman pressed her lips tightly, then sighed. "Fine. It's not like we're safe in these monster-infested streets anyway."

Darren nodded, then grasped the handle of his gun more tightly, took a deep breath, and stepped out of the alley. Quickly, they crossed the street, entered through the main gates, and started walking down the expansive meadow.

Darren's eyes were fixed on the demons, and his heart was pounding heavily in his chest. Since the initial attack on Daniel's palace, he tried his hardest to continue moving and focus on the mission ahead. That was the main thing that five years serving in Orox's militia had taught him, and it helped him keep his sanity despite the unimaginable horrors he had experienced. So, while his inner voice was screaming at him that he should save himself, his sense of duty prevailed, and he was ready to go to the depths of hell to rescue Daniel, his boss and long-time friend.

They were quickly approaching a set of steps ascending to an ajar entrance door. When they were just thirty yards away, the demon perching on the closest spire opened its eyes, released a loud screech, and soared into the sky before plummeting down, extending its sharp claws.

"Run!" Darren bellowed, then raised his pistol and fired three times, two bullets clipping the monster's wing and dropping the beast to the ground. Moments later, a cacophony of sharp screeches and bellows broke out as all the remaining demons awoke from their slumber and rose into the crimson sky, flapping their broad leathery wings before diving in the direction of the fleeing humans.

Christa grabbed Nina, ran up the stairs, and leaped inside, with Darren following behind them. After entering, the man slammed the door shut just in time before the demons could reach him. Then, the three rushed through the maze of long gloomy corridors illuminated by numerous ornate lanterns.

They stopped after a couple of minutes. Christa put Nina on the ground, then leaned on her knees, panting, looking warily at the expansive stained glass windows. "Won't they just crash through?" she muttered.

Darren rubbed his chin, then looked over his shoulder. "Well, they could've easily followed us through the door, but it seems that, for some reason, they're not willing to go inside."

Christa straightened her back, then hugged her shaking shoulders. "Something feels very wrong about this place."

"What do you mean?"

"Just look at all the blood," Christa motioned at the carpeted floor covered with a thick layer of gore. "Something horrible had happened here."

Darren sighed. "Well, there's no sense in speculating. Let's just find Daniel and Keri and leave."

He started creeping down the corridor with large windows on their left and an array of ornate oak doors on the right. He tried to remember the layout of the palace that his contact Jonathan had shown him some hours ago, which now felt like it was in another lifetime. While the man promised to help rescue Daniel from the holding cells, Darren supposed that it was safe to assume that he was likely to have perished along with the troops that tried to defend the city from the demonic onslaught.

As they moved toward the palace center, they observed an increasing amount of blood. It was splattered not only on the floor but also on the walls and the windows, and there were even a few red streaks on the high ceiling, the sight of which sent shivers down Darren's spine. There was also a large number of guns and bullet casings scattered throughout, indicating that an intense firefight had recently taken place. Still, they hadn't seen a single body, which gave rise to ghastly images in Darren's mind of horrific beasts feasting on the carcasses of their victims, devouring everything to the last bit.

He crouched down and grabbed one of the pistols, then quickly checked the magazine to see that it was half-full before extending it to Christa: "Here. Just in case."

The woman hesitated, looking at the bloodied handle, then took it before mumbling: "The guns didn't help these men; why do you think it would be different for us?"

Darren shrugged, then noticed a shotgun lying by the windowsill, partly hidden in the shadow of the wall. He grabbed the weapon and quickly examined it to find three rounds inside before swinging it over the shoulder and resuming ambling forward. He was about to turn around the corner when Nina scurried toward him and grabbed him by the sleeve. "We need to hide," she whispered. "*It* is coming."

The man was opening his mouth to ask what *it* was when he heard a distant wailing accompanied by strange rustling. Nina's blue eyes widened, and her face became as pale as paper. Still holding onto Darren's sleeve, she stepped toward the open door leading into one of the guest chambers. The man looked at Christa and was surprised to see that her face was even paler than Nina's, and her teeth were visibly chattering in her mouth. Meanwhile, the creepy rustling was quickly approaching, now accompanied by disgusting slurping and clicking.

As quietly as possible, the three sneaked inside the room. Darren was about to close the door, but Nina tugged on his sleeve again, then shook her head, looking at him intently. After lingering for another second, the man decided to follow the child's instincts, which somehow sensed whatever horror was shambling toward them.

They huddled in the furthest and darkest corner of the room and started to wait. Darren's heart was pounding as he watched with bated breath the shadow of some massive creature creep into the room. He could now discern at least ten separate voices moaning tearfully in unison. The monster seemed to be moving past them, but then it stopped.

Darren could feel Christa's body trembling as she stood with her hands covering her mouth, trying to stop her teeth from grinding in agitation. With wide eyes, he watched three slimy tentacles slither inside the room and start grabbing around. Then, the stench of utmost putridness assaulted his sense of smell, and he just barely stopped himself from hurling by pressing his hands to his mouth, mirroring Christa beside him.

The writhing appendages continued to reach around, smearing the floor and the walls with disgusting goo. As uneasy seconds slowly crawled by, the room seemed to shrink, and Darren kept pressing his back against the wall, his eyes locked on the slowly approaching limbs.

Suddenly, a monstrous scream came from outside. Darren heard Christa's muffled whimper, and he turned to her with his eyes wide with terror. But thankfully, the entity didn't seem to notice it through the infernal bellow that, for several seconds, engulfed the entire continent.

After the echos of the beastly voice grew quiet, Darren was relieved to see the tentacles retracting. Then, he heard the creepy wailing of numerous voices again as the beast started quickly shambling away from the door, seemingly going in the direction they came from.

The three stood unmovingly, still trying to make as little sound as possible, peering at the crimson light falling through the open door. Then, after they could no longer hear the grumblings of the entity, Darren finally stepped out of the corner and started inching his way toward the door.

"Darren," he heard Christa's trembling voice and turned to see her still standing with her back pressed against the wall.

"I think we should go before that thing comes back," the man muttered. "We need to rescue Daniel before it makes its way to the holding cells."

"I think that thing *was* Daniel," Christa whispered. "This happened to him before, back in Pentara. He turned into a tentacled demon and consumed everyone in the prison. Keri was the one who helped him regain his human form."

Darren opened his mouth, then closed it again, unable to find the words to describe the bafflement that Christa's statement had brought. His first thought was that the woman had gone crazy from terror. Then, he started wondering if she was saying such things to make him leave. However, as the eerie seconds passed, more and more macabre ideas began to surface in his mind.

What if she's telling the truth? Is it really that far-fetched, considering everything that had happened? Even if she isn't, what are the chances that this monster killed everyone in the palace but left Daniel and Keri alive?

The man gritted his teeth, then took another step toward the door, trying to avoid the disgusting sludge smeared on the floor. Doubt was slowly creeping into his quivering mind. The walls that his sanity tried to hide behind were crumbling. With the future course of action no longer clear, he found himself in a horrible predicament: continue on his mission, hoping to find his boss alive against all odds or flee and have a better chance at saving himself but at the cost of the remnants of his sane mind.

After a few uneasy seconds, Christa finally left the corner and approached him while holding Nina by the hand.

"You think we should leave?" Darren asked, looking at the woman intently.

"We can't leave before we save Keri," Nina whimpered.

Darren shifted his eyes toward her, then glanced at the door before releasing a deep sigh, deciding to grab onto their only lead, despite its bizarre implications. "Do you know where she is?" the man asked. "Can you... feel her, like you felt the monster?"

Nina lowered her eyes briefly, then gave Darren a little nod. "She's upstairs, locked in a small room. The monsters haven't gotten to her yet, but now it's only a matter of time."

"What about Daniel?"

The girl pressed her lips tightly, keeping her eyes low. "We need to rescue Keri," she mumbled. "The lady in white told me that she is our only hope of saving the world."

Daniel glanced at Christa, standing with an undecipherable expression on her face, her eyes staring blankly before her as if she was on the verge of becoming catatonic. He then knelt beside Nina, placing his hands on the girl's shoulders and looking into her eyes. "We can go to Keri as soon as we free Daniel, okay? I know he can't be that far away from where we are now, but I can't remember the exact layout of this place. Could you take me to him?"

"But—"

"We need Daniel to help us fight off the monsters," Darren said. "Could you help us, sweetie? Please."

Nina looked at him warily for a bit longer, then finally nodded, let go of Christa's hand, and stepped out of the room. The woman followed her with the same blank expression, seemingly lost in her dark thoughts. Darren joined them, and they started walking down the wide corridor partly covered in slime, slowly seeping into the blood-drenched floor and producing the concoction of utmost putridness.

Like Darren predicted, it only took them several minutes before they reached a set of steps leading toward the narrow passageway that took them to the arched oak door. Darren grabbed the handle and tried to open it, but unfortunately, it was locked.

"God damn it," he mumbled, then glanced at Christa and Nina. "Step back, you two."

"What are you going to do, mister?" the girl asked while Christa was still staring blankly into nowhere.

"Whatever it takes to save my friend," Darren said, then grabbed his shotgun and aimed it at the lock.

"No," Nina whimpered. "*It* will hear us. We need to get to Keri first."

She stepped forward, grabbing Darren's pants, but he pushed the girl away, then gripped the gun handle more tightly and pressed the trigger.

A loud bang pierced the eerie tranquility, followed by a faint thud as the pellets slammed into the wood, sending splinters in all directions and shattering part of the lock. Ignoring Nina's whimpers, Darren stepped forward, kicked the door open, and walked into a wide chamber with twenty holding cells illuminated by several dim lanterns hanging from the stone ceiling.

After scanning the room, Darren saw a frail red-haired woman standing in the furthest cell on the right. He quickly approached, widening his eyes after seeing Daniel lying in the cell across from her. The man had a large gash on top of his head, and most of his face was severely swollen, with his eyes tightly shut.

"Mister, we need to go!" Nina screamed. "The monster is coming!"

Ignoring her pleas, Darren aimed the barrel at the lock of Daniel's cell and fired another shot, which echoed loudly in the room and flung the metal door open. The man then glanced toward the woman in the other cell, who took a step away from the bars, looking at him intently with her glinty gray eyes. He then remembered that there was only one round remaining in the gun. "Sorry," he mumbled, then slung the shotgun over his shoulder, stepped into Daniel's cell, and grabbed the man from the ground.

Suddenly, an ear-piercing shriek enveloped the chamber. Darren quickly turned to see Christa standing by the door, trying desperately to escape two tentacles wrapped around her legs. Hurriedly, he put Daniel back on the ground, then rushed out of the cell, grabbed his pistol, and started shooting at the slimy appendages until they let the woman go. Wailing and whimpering, she retreated to the back of the room, cowering by the wall. Meanwhile, Darren took a step closer to see more tentacles slithering across the corridor.

As he peered into the scarlet twilight, his eyes widened, and a gasp escaped his throat as he saw a horrific abomination standing on the other end of the narrow passageway, trying to squeeze through. It looked like an amalgamation of quivering flesh with ghoulish bodies hanging from its sides, their faces distorted by utmost anguish. Among them, Darren saw his contact Johnathan with his bloodshot eyes bulging from their sockets.

Suddenly, Johnathan's expression changed, and his blue lips twisted into a horrific grin. Then, he opened his mouth and spoke in a croaky gargling voice: "Come forth and join us, Darren. The pain will only last for a few seconds, and then, it will all be over. You'll become a part of something bigger, and together, we'll push back the terror screaming at the sea and pave the path for a new world."

Darren stepped back, his hands holding the pistol trembling and his heart pounding heavily in his chest. His mind was now filled with grisly visions of the lands Beyond filled with ghouls and grotesque misshapen beings. He looked back at Christa and Nina, cowering at the back of the room. He then glanced at the pistol in his hand, deliberating whether to press it to his temple and pull the trigger in order to escape the nightmare unfolding before him.

Meanwhile, Johnathan's creepy smirk became even broader as he turned his bloodshot eyes to the red-headed woman standing in the cell before speaking again: "This invitation extends to all of you: Eliza, Christa, and little Nina. Come forth and join us. Come forth and accept the gift given to us by the immortal will of the one who lurks between the seams. Come forth and submit your flesh to the Corpse Crawler – the blackest abyss of the universe."

Keri

Keri was awoken by a hoarse metallic bellow. She shuddered and opened her eyes to see that she was sitting inside a boxy cabin. She then turned her head and looked out the foggy window at the tall mountains of the Restless Peaks, slowly moving past her.

Keri rubbed her eyes and released a deep sigh, trying to remember the strange dream she had, but her mind was covered by a thick fog. Her gaze shifted to the leather backpack lying beside her. She then extended her pale arm, pulled a slightly crumpled sheet of paper out of the pocket, and looked at hurriedly written squiggly letters.

Dear Keri,

Even while writing this, I'm still agonizing about whether to take my piteous infatuation to THE DEEPEST PITS OF HELL. However, as I SCREAM IN ETERNAL ANGUISH, I keep wishing for nothing else but to gaze upon your fair face again.

I keep reminiscing about those blissful days we spent together playing in the fields of my fathers, giggling and joking around in our childish naivety. I keep wondering about what could have been if I had joined you on that fated day when you slammed the doors and left our village for the prospect of greater happiness in the bustling Heart of Talos. HOW DID THAT WORK OUT, BY THE WAY?

I will not deny that I held the grievance for said abandonment, YOU SELFISH SHREW, but my time is running short, and I can not afford to hold on to my pettiness anymore.

Thus, I'm writing this letter to you in the faint hope of forgiveness, and if you would be as so kind as to be able to find such feeling in the bottom of your heart, maybe you would be willing to STEP INTO THE LAKE OF FIRE? I'll understand if you won't, and I swear that I will not harness any malign thought, as even in my dying moment, you will always remain my sweet, beloved STRUGGLER.

Sincerely,
Nathaniel

Keri sighed, then glanced at the address on the other side of the letter: Lynn, the village of the damned, a pile of ashes where the central barn used to be. "Poor Nathaniel," she mumbled before shifting her gaze out the window.

Several minutes later, the train bellowed one last time and started to slow down, approaching the Exter's railway station. Keri got up, threw on her backpack, and began walking toward the exit, looking at the people sitting in the other cabins. There were men, women, and children, all dressed in ragged clothes and staring silently before them from their sunken, ghoulish faces. Some of them seemed vaguely familiar, especially a group just by the exit, wearing worn-down police uniforms, although Keri couldn't recall exactly where she had seen them before.

The train finally stopped, and the large metal door opened, allowing Keri to exit. She saw a group of people with coal-stained clothes waiting outside, huddled closely in Exter's tiny railway station. In front of them stood a muscular woman with long curly hair. She stepped to the open door, then turned toward the rest and spoke in a clear, cheerful voice: "Alright, everyone, hop in! Quickly! You don't want to be left behind, do you?"

The people started boarding the train, many holding pickaxes, hammers, and chisels, while the burly woman watched them intently. "Avie, where are you!?" she hollered, extending her neck.

"Over here!" a man in the crowd raised his arm, then hurried upfront.

"Why are you hiding from me, you rascal?" the woman grumbled. After the man shrugged apologetically, she sighed, then added: "Alright, hop in. Save me a seat."

From the crusty meadow, Keri watched the miners board the train. The burly woman was the last to go. She looked over her shoulder, giving Keri a faint smile before uttering: "Good luck." She then turned and disappeared inside the bowels of the metallic monstrosity that was beginning to bellow again, announcing its departure.

Keri lingered a bit longer, then started walking down a rough stone road ascending a short hill. She tilted her head up, letting her pale face bask in the bright illumination of the blood moon as she strolled onward, whistling a faint melody under her breath.

Suddenly, a young man emerged at the top of the hill wearing a brown leather jacket and holding a large bag. After seeing the train, his eyes widened, and a gasp escaped his mouth. "Alexa, hurry up!" he shouted, then looked over his shoulder.

Soon, a bespectacled woman with curly brown hair appeared, wearing a black denim jacket, baggy blue pants, and black leather shoes. She also gasped, then they started running downhill, holding hands, their clothes fluttering in the wind. "You just had to take another peek at the castle!" Keri heard the woman complain as they ran past her.

The metallic beast bellowed again, and for a moment, it looked like the two weren't going to make it. Yet, they hopped inside just before the metal door slammed shut. Seconds later, the train started moving, and Keri watched it approach the dense grove looming in the distance. She then sighed, turned, and resumed her amble.

After she ascended the hill, a bleak vista opened before her eyes of the scarlet waters of Dilos outstretching to the horizon with massive waves slamming onto the rocky shore. Beside it stood the desolate town of Exter, most of its buildings turned into rubble by decades of decay and neglect. In the distance, she could also see a solitary ivory tower, the remnant of the massive castle that once loomed over the land.

Keri hesitated. Her eyes trembled as an immense yearning washed over her, its cause still hidden by a thick fog covering her mind. She sighed, then entered the town and started walking down a dusty road, her black platform shoes clicking eerily on the stony surface.

As she approached the town center, she heard the joyful laughter of children, and soon she saw at least fifty of them playing among the rubble of a large building surrounded by a fence. They were watched by a tall woman in a long gray dress wearing a harlequin scarf on her head. After noticing Keri, she gave her a wary look while crossing her hands over her chest.

They gazed at each other for a bit. Then, Keri resumed walking, moving toward the eastern side of the town, still trying desperately to recall the reason for the yearning that was making her eyes water and her heart flutter uncomfortably in her chest. Soon, she saw three men standing outside the old building with a caved-in roof with a sign reading "Miner's Tavern" lying on the ground.

"What do you mean there are no funds for repairs, Gustav?" she heard a portly man with a thick mustache say to a tall man with a short black beard. "After the miners and the Wyrms left, my tavern is the only thing keeping this town afloat."

"We don't even have enough resources to repair the communal buildings, Dante," Gustav said, then sighed, turning to the third man with a patch of sparse gray hair on his head. "The same goes for you, Gerald: if you want to fix your hotel, you'll just have to do it yourself."

Gerald spat to the side and grumbled: "God damn it, Gustav. What am I supposed to do if the tourists show up?"

"Well, I wouldn't worry about that," Gustav said, then sighed deeply before adding: "That was the last train."

Keri looked at the three men for a bit longer, then finally approached them. "Excuse me," she said shyly while raising her hand.

The men turned, looking at her wide-eyed, seemingly startled by her presence.

"Could you point me to the road to Lynn?" Keri asked.

The men shared glances with one another. Then, Gustav took a step forward and said: "Well, there's only one road going out of here, Miss." He raised his arm, pointing at the dusty road outstretching toward the distant mountains. "But I wouldn't go to that place if I were you. The only thing you'll find in Lynn is the spirits of the past, wailing in their eternal anguish."

"I need to go there to see my friend."

"Why don't you stay here with us?" Dante suggested, giving her a friendly smile. "I have a cellar filled with Exter's finest wine and ale. Enough to help you forget whatever worry is burdening your heart."

"Thank you, but I can't," Keri said, shaking her head. "My friend is waiting for me. This might be my last opportunity to see him."

"Well, go on then," Gerald grumbled bitterly while motioning with his scrawny hand. "But you ought to hurry up. The night is coming, and you don't want to get caught wandering the mountains past the witching hour."

Keri bit her lower lip, then raised her eyes to the blood moon with the contours of a creepy misshapen face on its surface. A shiver ran down her spine, and she hugged her shoulders, suddenly feeling cold. Then, she thanked the men and started quickly heading down the narrow pathway leading away from the city.

After walking for about fifty yards, Keri looked over her shoulder to see the men still staring at her. Their figures in the crimson dusk appeared faded and twisted as if they were not humans but apparitions of wicked ghouls. She shuddered and quickened her step, her eyes fixed on the distant mountains.

Keri passed an abandoned mine with a wisp of smoke rising from its entrance, obscured by layers of rubble. Then, she stepped into the mountain pass, listening to the wind howling eerily between the high peaks.

It was slowly getting darker as she ambled hurriedly down the rough pathway zigzagging around the steep rocks. There were narrow roads leading into the valleys laden with strange misshapen idols built from wood and stone, tied together with a hemp rope. However, Keri resisted the temptation to observe them up close and kept moving forward, averting her gaze from their shadowy figures.

The road took a sharp turn. After stepping from behind the massive hill, Keri saw a woman standing in the middle of the road, wearing a hospital gown, looking blankly before her. Keri hesitated for a few uneasy seconds, then stepped closer and spoke: "Hello? Are you lost?"

The woman slowly turned, her curly brown hair fluttering in the wind. She raised her arm and rubbed her earlobe, her red nails glinting in the twilight, then mumbled: "I'm looking for someone."

"I came from Exter, but I haven't met anyone along the way," Keri said.

The woman shook her head. "He must be somewhere in these mountains. I know it. Edgar wouldn't just leave me out here alone."

"Why don't you come with me? I'll bring you to my village. Maybe people there can help you."

The woman's eyes widened. "Village? There's no village or anything else beyond these mountains. Only the veil of darkness. I need to find Edgar before it engulfs us all."

Mumbling something incoherently, the woman quickly walked past and disappeared behind the corner. After looking in the direction of her leaving for a bit longer, Keri resumed ambling forward, feeling increasingly uneasy. Some of her memories were beginning to surface as a jumble of faces, names, and gruesome scenes of slaughter. Although Keri couldn't yet piece them together, these images were clear enough to deduce that the world before her was far from what it seemed.

Something definitely had happened between me boarding the train in Atheta and waking up a few hours ago. Could this still be a dream? But who are these people I see in my head, and why does looking at them cause me so much anguish?

Captured in her brooding, Keri didn't even notice how the mountains parted, and she almost ended up tumbling down a steep cliff. Thankfully, she caught herself at the last second and quickly stepped back before tilting her head, looking at a desolate plain of black rock stretching before her.

Keri gasped a few times, feeling sadness rising from within as she remembered the colorful meadows and dense vegetation that served as a playground for Lynn's children. But now, there was nothing but naked dead trees protruding awkwardly from the dry, cracked ground.

Keri lingered for a while longer, then, on shaky legs, descended into the desolate plain and started walking forward, her footsteps rustling eerily in the surrounding silence. It was quickly getting darker, and the face on the moon was now clearly visible with its bulging eyes and broad mouth filled with sharp fangs. While Keri tried not to look at the cosmic abomination hovering above, she could feel its ravenous leer watching her closely, exacerbating her growing dread.

Shortly, the remnants of her home village emerged in the distance. After getting closer, Keri stopped, released a short sob, then crumbled to her knees, looking at the charred carcasses of once-familiar buildings. "I don't understand," she whimpered. "What could've happened? What the hell is going on?"

"Lots of things had happened."

Keri shuddered and turned her head to see Nathaniel standing ten yards away, his black hair riddled with gray strands and his visage sunken and wrinkled.

"I didn't think I'll ever see you again," the man said hoarsely.

Keri got up, looking intently into his bloodshot eyes. "Nathaniel, what is going on?"

"My weakness and self-pity had brought the curse upon this world. My spirit is already lost, and I am damned to wander the black waste for aeons to come. But you, Keri, still hold a glimmer of hope. All you have to do is remember what brought you to this point and embrace your role as the spark that will illuminate the somber skies and vanquish the mad Ancients back into their cosmic slumber."

Keri lowered her eyes. "I'm not sure if I want to remember."

"Then the darkness will engulf the entire world, and all those who still struggle will disappear in the insatiable Maw of the Hollow." Nathaniel sighed, then added: "Nevertheless, the choice is yours. You bear no obligation to sacrifice yourself to undo my blasphemous act."

The man sighed again, then turned and started ambling toward the crimson-soaked horizon. As Keri looked at his receding figure, memories flooded her mind, accompanied by a plethora of emotions ranging from angst to utmost dismay. "It's not your fault, Nathaniel!" she shouted, tears welling in her eyes.

The man paused for a split second, then gave her one last glance before resuming his amble. Gradually, his outline faded away, blending into the spectral twilight, and Keri was left standing alone between the ruins of Lynn village.

After lingering for a bit longer, she turned and started walking across the empty streets, more memories now rising from the darkness of her mind of both her childhood days and her horrid encounters with the eldritch beasts.

"With so many lives gone, can humanity really recover? Even if we somehow pushed the demons back, could we rebuild what was lost? Or would our victory only be temporary, and corruption would eventually spread again, swallowing those who somehow managed to live through these dreadful times?"

From somewhere came a lone gust of wind, carrying a sorrowful sob of a small child. Keri paused, then started quickly walking in the direction of the sound. Shortly, she left the ruins of Lynn and continued through the black waste toward a dense forest looming in the distance, somehow untouched by the decay and destruction surrounding it.

With her heart pounding, Keri entered the thicket, following the distant sobs. She trudged through the dense vegetation, ignoring thorny shrubs and tall weeds, cutting her skin and drawing blood.

Keri didn't know how much time had passed as she kept pushing forward, huffing and puffing, sweat rolling from her forehead and mixing with blood seeping from numerous tiny cuts on her flesh. Eventually, she saw a faint yellow light glistening in the distance.

She stepped into a small clearing with a massive stone in the middle riddled with intricate ornaments covered partly by blue moss and small yellow-petaled flowers. In front of the stone stood Sila, grasping a large lantern, her black cloak and yellow hair fluttering in the wind and a broad smile shining on her dainty-featured face. Beside her, leaning against the stone, was a little girl with very long black hair reaching to her knees and covering most of her face.

"Welcome, Keri," the witch spoke softly. "It has been a long journey, but you're finally here – at the edge of the universe."

Keeping her sky-blue eye on Keri, Sila turned and swiped across the stone with her pale hand, producing a myriad of multicolored sparks that glistened brightly in the surrounding dark. Seconds later, the air in the clearing thickened, resonating with a loud hum.

"What is the meaning of this?" Keri asked, her gaze shifting from the witch to the child beside her.

"You've proven yourself to be worthy to peer beyond the veil," Sila said, broadening her smile. "You triumphed over numerous perilous challenges – a testament to your indomitable spirit. Now, only the final step remains before you enter the Eternal Halls and bask in the ethereal radiance of the Old Ones."

"You're a liar, Sila," Keri snarled. "I don't believe a single word coming out of your vile mouth. I don't know what you have planned now, but, like always, your efforts will fail."

"Fail?" Sila chuckled. "The fact that you're standing before me is a testament to the resounding success of my endeavors in this humble realm."

Keri grabbed the bag from her shoulders and started rummaging through it, searching for her revolver. Meanwhile, Sila continued: "I said to you back in Exter that your existence is precious, for you were once a part of me, born in the void of the cosmos."

"A part of you?" Keri asked. Unable to find her weapon, she dropped her bag and started looking around the clearing for a stone or some sharp object she could use to bash the witch's brains in before her wicked tongue could poison her mind.

"When the gods shine, tiny pieces of their essence break off and spread throughout the hollow. While most of these specs fade into nothing, some give rise to extraordinary beings. And you are it, Keri, the spawn of my wondrous gleam, found amidst the dense forest during the darkest night and raised by the residents of Lynn. It has come time for you to return where you belong and soar beside me through the shimmering darkness of the void."

Sila stepped forward, extending her hands as if inviting Keri for a hug. "Come, my child. Your struggles have come to an end. Come, and I will erase the mark that binds your sacred soul."

"Come with us, Keri," the girl spoke, also taking a step closer. The light from the lantern in Sila's hand revealed her glinty green eyes peering out of a frail visage that seemed strangely familiar to Keri as if she was looking at a long-lost friend.

Peering at the girl and the mesmerizing gleam coming from Sila's eye, an overwhelming desire washed over her to follow the witch into whatever realm she would choose to guide her. But then, the faces arose in her mind's eye of Eliza, of her crew, of Leonard and Alistair, of Daniel, Christa, and Nina, and many others who fell in the fight against the forces of the Beyond.

"What about the others?" Keri asked. "What about those still fighting and those who perished but are trapped in purgatory by the wicked curse you brought into this world?"

"Why do you care about those insignificant dots in the sky?" Sila asked. "The Great Eye of Creation can summon billions of them in a single blink."

"They are not insignificant!" Keri exclaimed. "They all have hopes and aspirations. They all have paths they want to follow. And their shining can be just as bright as the one of the Ancients that you keep blabbering about. So go back to whatever dark hole you crawled out of because I'll never join the likes of you!"

The smile finally disappeared from Sila's face, and she lowered her arms. Meanwhile, the girl beside her started sobbing, big scarlet tears rolling down her cheeks.

"Now look what you've done!" Sila exclaimed, rage suddenly distorting her beauteous face. She stepped forward, grabbed the patch covering her eye, and lifted it to reveal an empty hole filled with a bright emerald gleam. "I'm done playing games with you. One way or the other, you're coming with me."

Keri wobbled, feeling like she was being sucked into the expansion of shimmering green light that quickly enveloped everything around. She felt her strength fading and her memories sinking into oblivion as she tried to avert her gaze but couldn't even move a muscle, shackled by otherworldly energy slowly permeating her essence.

Sila extended her arm and grabbed Keri by the wrist. At that moment, everything was engulfed by a bright white light, pushing away the emerald gleam. The witch gasped and withdrew, then turned her gaze to the giant gap in space opening behind her. Then came the clanging of chains, which made Sila stagger before grabbing her ears. Gritting her teeth, she glared at Keri, then spoke in a voice filled with utmost contempt: "You think that your world will be saved by some long-forgotten deity who's too afraid of entropy to leave its confined realm? Fine then! Perish with the rest of them!"

Sila and the girl faded out of sight. For a while, Keri floated in that boundless expansion of bright light filled with eerie echoes speaking in a language she could not understand. Then, she felt a sharp pain surging through her body, and she turned her head to see that in place of her right hand was nothing but a gory stump.

Keri gasped, then sat up and looked around a narrow hospital room illuminated by a single yellow lamp hanging above the large door. She coughed a few times, feeling sharp pain surging through her chest, then turned, lifting her numb feet out of bed.

She lingered for a bit, gripping the edge with her remaining hand, then took a deep breath and stood up. Her bones crackled, and she winced from many aches in her battered flesh but somehow managed to keep herself from falling. Then, she ambled across the room, put her hand on the handle, and pushed.

Her eyes peered upon the crimson light falling through the large windows in the corridor ahead. Seconds later, she heard a ferocious scream and felt her eyes lighting up with the bright emerald light. Despite her sorry condition, the powers within her seemed more eager than ever to step into the shadow and face the beast threatening to swallow her world.

For a second, the corridor disappeared, and she saw Nina and Christa cowering in the corner, trying to keep away from numerous tentacles creeping into the room with twenty holding cells. After the vision faded, Keri gritted her teeth, feeling the otherworldly energy pulsating in every molecule of her being. She then started shambling toward the distant steps, her mind finally void of fear and hesitation, ready to take on the eldritch beasts again.

Eliza

The lock-up was enveloped by wailings and bellows of the monster mixed with Christa's incessant shrieking. Darren stood several yards from the back of the room, flailing his rifle at the bleeding tentacles trying to snatch him away. For a split second, Eliza was afraid that he might try to take an easy way out, but he ended up emptying his weapons into the writhing limbs, forcing a few of them to retract. However, more and more of them were slithering into the room, covering the floor, the walls, and even the ceiling with a quivering fleshy mess that reeked of rot and decay, making Eliza want to hurl out her insides.

She grabbed onto the bars of her cell and pulled a few times in desperation, looking at Christa's horrified face as she was pushing against the wall as if wanting to go through to escape the slowly but surely approaching madness.

Suddenly, several tentacles shot forward, wrapping around Darren's ankles and making him tumble. The man screamed, then started bashing the quivering limbs with the end of his shotgun, but more of them shot forward, entangling his arms and starting to drag him out of the room.

"God damn it!" the man screamed, terror permeating his voice as he tried to escape. "God damn it all! God—"

His bellows turned into hoarse gargles as one of the tentacles wrapped around his neck and began squeezing. Eliza watched it all in terror, wondering whether she was also destined for the same horrid fate.

The tentacles will reach through the bars, wrap around me, and drag me out, breaking my limbs and bones in the process. I'll probably feel every second of it, and by the end, I'll be begging the beast lurking outside the room to alleviate my bodily sufferings by devouring me whole.

Perhaps I should've agreed to Sila's request and unleashed Dagon's army upon this world, making the monsters fight each other. What's the point of resisting if everything's already lost?

As Eliza watched the man being dragged away, the little girl, whom Eliza heard being called Nina, got out of Christa's fearful embrace, then rushed forward and released a loud shriek, her eyes gleaming with emerald light.

A couple of tentacles exploded, and the rest grew limp, allowing Darren to escape their grasp. He turned his head, wheezing, looking at the girl, his gaze full of horror and bafflement. Meanwhile, Nina's eyes rolled upward, and she wobbled before dropping heavily to the ground, her head bouncing off the rough surface and opening a wide gash that immediately started leaking blood.

Darren rushed to the girl and grabbed her into his arms. He then turned and released a hoarse gasp before retreating to the back of the room next to Christa, whose shrieks and wails now turned into desperate, barely audible whimpers as she lay curled into a ball, hugging her own knees and rocking back and forth.

Eliza watched the three briefly, then turned her eyes in the direction of Darren's widened gaze. Soon, she heard strange rustling accompanied by disgusting slurping and rattling. Then, at the back of the corridor appeared several grotesque bodies conjoined at the waist, protruding from some fleshy mass. The ghouls were grabbing the walls with their bony hands, slowly squeezing through the narrow corridor, covering it with blood and gore.

"No one can escape the blackest abyss," one of the monsters grumbled, its jaw moving up and down uncannily. "No one can escape the Corpse Crawler. Soon, you'll have the privilege of sharing your flesh with the god of all gods for the rest of eternity."

After releasing a horrible screech, the entity lunged forward, finally making its way inside the room, revealing its horrific form consisting of chunks of flesh with ghoulish bodies hanging from the sides, some of them crushed by the walls of the corridor, wailing horribly as blood and guts leaked out of their deformed bodies.

Christa started shrieking again while Darren just stared, holding unconscious Nina in his hands, his face slowly turning pale and his mouth moving without producing any sound. Meanwhile, the monster's tentacles started moving again, gripping the surface and slowly pushing the rest of the grotesque body forward as the ghoul that spoke before opened its mouth and started cackling madly.

The beastly limbs were about to wrap around Christa, Nina, and Darren when the entire room was engulfed by emerald light. Eliza covered her eyes, blinded by the bright gleam. Then, she heard a horrific roar, followed by a wet splattering sound.

Once she regained her vision, Eliza was presented with a gruesome sight: the floor was covered in a gooey mass riddled with remnants of corpses and numerous tentacles, devoid of their previous vigor and twitching in postmortem convulsions. In the center of all that disgusting mess lay Kyron, naked, his wide-open eyes peering blankly at the ceiling.

An eerie silence descended on the room. Then, Eliza heard something rustling in the corridor, and she shifted her eyes just as Keri entered through the doorway, wearing a hospital gown. Her face was ashen, and it seemed like she was barely standing on her feet, but her eyes gleamed with a ferocious determination that Eliza hadn't seen before.

"Keri!" Nina's thin voice pierced the uncomfortable silence. The girl escaped Darren's grasp and sloshed across the room through the gooey mess before giving Keri's waist a tight hug.

The woman smiled faintly and patted the girl on the head. Then, she quickly scanned the room and spoke in a tired, hoarse voice: "I need to get to the Dilos Sea. Could one of you help me? I don't think we have enough time for me to get there by myself."

Without hesitation, Eliza stepped forward, feeling tears welling in her eyes. "I'll do it," she said. "Someone just needs to get me out of this damn cell."

"I'll also come," Darren uttered. "I have no idea what's going on, but as long as you have some kind of a plan, it's better than just sitting and waiting for those ghouls to get us."

"You fools!" Kyron's thunderous voice pierced the room as the man pushed off the ground and stood up, disgusting sludge dripping from his bare skin. "What have you done!?"

The man looked around, his eyes wide and body trembling from anger. "This was our only shot! Only united as one could we have challenged the horror that is about to enter this world. And now it's all over! And for what?"

"Just shut the hell up!"

Eliza turned to see Daniel slowly rising from the ground, grasping the bars of his cell. "Don't you understand that you've been tricked by that beast?" the man said. "If not for Keri, all of our spirits would be eternally trapped in the domain of suffering."

"How dare you talk to me like that!" Kyron bellowed and stepped toward Daniel, but Darren rushed forward to block his way.

"We don't have time to argue!" Keri exclaimed, power radiating from her voice, making everyone turn their attention toward her. "The hour is late, and the beast is about to rise."

Darren gave Kyron another contemptuous look, then grabbed his shotgun and started bashing the door of Eliza's cell. After about a minute, the lock finally gave out, allowing her to exit. She rushed to Keri, hugging her gently and giving her cheek a heartfelt kiss before whispering: "I didn't think I'd ever see you again."

"You and me both," Keri said, giving her an intent look before turning back to the other people in the room. "The rest of you should barricade in the palace and wait until this is over. One way or the other."

"Not a chance," Daniel said, giving her a faint smirk that distorted his battered face. "I've never backed down from any foe, and I'm not about to start now. I'm seeing this thing through the end."

"I hate to agree with this man, but I feel the same way," Kyron grumbled. "If you plan to make some kind of a last stand, I would be willing to put our differences aside."

"Are we really going to trust this old geezer after he slaughtered all his men and tried to kill us?!" Darren spouted.

"I would not be willing to," Daniel said. "But unfortunately, I had succumbed to the same infernal temptation back in Pentara. The demon that had convinced him to do all those things is a master at manipulating the minds of those lustful for power."

"I'm also going with you, guys," Christa whimpered, finally able to get a hold of herself. "I don't want to be left here alone."

"Fine, let's just move – we don't have time to chat," Keri said, then turned, exited the room, and started hobbling down the corridor.

Eliza joined her, holding Keri's hand and helping her to push forward. Meanwhile, Nina walked just behind them, followed by Christa, Darren, and Daniel, who was wincing with every step. Kyron walked in the back, his body covered in dirty rags that he found in the corner of one of the unoccupied cells.

Before leaving the palace, they armed themselves with weapons scattered across the wide hallways. Eliza grabbed a pistol for herself and offered another one to Keri, but she refused, saying that weapons won't do much good against the foe they were about to face. A few minutes later, they stopped by the main entrance.

"Careful, there are demons perched on the spires," Darren said. "We'll likely need to make a run for it."

"You don't need to worry about those monsters anymore," Keri said. "I'll take care of everything. You just stay in the back."

The group traded glances with one another but didn't argue. As soon as they pushed the door open, they heard a cacophony of shrieks and screeches as dozens of winged creatures plunged from above, extending their sharp claws and baring their fangs.

Eliza was about to start firing when Keri pushed her away, then stepped forward and raised her hand. Moments later, her eyes lit up, and a bright emerald gleam enveloped everything again, piercing through the crimson illumination falling from above.

Once the light faded, Eliza saw charred demonic bodies falling to the ground. They smashed into the crusty meadow, shattering into tiny pieces of ash and cinder that were scattered by the strong gust of wind that came seemingly out of nowhere, drowning everything in its tearful howl.

The group lingered briefly, captured in fearful awe. All except for Nina, who was the first to follow Keri out of the palace. Eliza noticed that the gash on the girl's head had already closed up, leaving only a tiny mark. Looking at the two, she wondered whether they were still human or if they had become nothing but a catalyst for humanity's conjoined will.

"There is a truck parked outside," Darren said. He exited the palace, then, taking broad, quick steps, crossed the paved pathway leading to the large gates with the rest of the group following behind him.

Soon, they hopped inside a large military truck with Darren and Keri in front and the rest of the group huddled in the back. It took several minutes for the man to hot-wire the car. Then, they took off and drove across the inner city, past the wall, and into the main road while Keri, using her newfound abilities, shielded them from the numerous demons, monsters, and ghouls that tried to thwart their advance.

Faye

She could already see the waters of Dilos glistening on the horizon and the peaks of tall buildings of Kebury Port. Faye kept looking over her shoulder while grasping the obsidian sword in her hand. Although she could not yet see the beast, she could feel its eyes leering at her from the shadows and sometimes hear muffled growls and barks carried by the cold wind.

The wound on her leg where Sofia sank her knife was throbbing, sending jolts of pain every step she took. And she could also feel some malady spreading throughout her body, beginning to numb her senses and blur her vision. Still, Faye pushed forward, desperate to save her life, even if the rest of the world was already lost.

As long as I'm still moving, there is still hope left. I have no reason to believe that the same horrors are unfolding in Talos. And even if they are, I can stock on resources and sail to the south – maybe try to wait it out in one of the islands of the Nameless Ocean. The military will sooner or later deal with whatever is happening… right?

Faye stepped into the empty streets and continued limping to the west – toward the docks. Like Dahbus, Kebury Port was in complete ruin: most of the buildings were crumbling, there were car wrecks everywhere, and the pavement was soaked with blood, guts, and dismembered body parts.

A strong gust of wind blew past her, sending shivers down her spine. In its cold embrace, it carried the vile stench of rot and decay and the already-familiar growl, which was seemingly getting closer. Faye looked over her shoulder, then nervously rubbed her nose before resuming her hobble.

Suddenly, she heard a ferocious roar and quickly turned to see a large brown-furred beast rushing at her at full speed. She gasped, then swung with her sword. The creature dodged, then roared again, exposing its sharp fangs, its yellow eyes full of rage and contempt. Then, from the depths of the grisly maw came a croaky female voice: "I'll tear open your belly and make you eat your insides for what you've done to my sister. I'll rip you to shreds, you murdering shrew!"

Faye gasped and took a step back. "Julie? Is that you?"

"I'll skin you alive and drag you to the deepest pits of hell where you'll burn in the infernal flames for the aeons to come!"

Julie lunged forward, gnashing her fangs. Faye stepped back, swinging the sword wildly, but the beast dodged again before biting into the woman's shoulder.

Faye shrieked. A sharp pain surged through her hand, her fingers trembled, and she almost lost hold of her sword. However, she regained control at the last second, gritting her teeth and drawing whatever strength remained in her abused body. Then, she raised her hand, looking the beast in the eyes, and thrust the blade through its chest, splattering its thick blood.

The creature released Faye's shoulder. She stepped back, withdrawing her sword from the beastly flesh. Meanwhile, the wolfman staggered backward, gargled something as if trying to speak, then dropped to the ground and convulsed several times before going limp.

Faye stood still for a while, panting, feeling blood leaking from her shoulder, as she peered at the corpse of the beast that not so long ago was just a scared woman, not that much different from herself. Then slowly, Faye turned her head, looking at her gory wound. In her mind, images arose of Julie's injury inflicted upon her during the confrontation with the wolfmen in Dahbus.

Will I also become the rage-filled abomination wandering these desolate lands? And if that's the case, is there any point in trying to flee? Should I accept my grim fate or keep going?

Faye gritted her teeth, then screamed in dismay-filled anguish: "How did it get to this?! Were the sins I've committed really so great to deserve the tortures of the damned?"

She released an angry shriek that echoed throughout the empty streets. Then, she started shambling toward the docks, the tip of the sword dragging on the pavement, producing an eerie screech. The backpack strap dug painfully into her injured shoulder, and she deliberated whether to throw the cursed thing away. However, in the end, she decided against it.

This is my burden. This backpack is where it all started. When I noticed that foreign woman carrying it in the bus station, and decided she would be an easy target. If I throw it away, I'll have nothing left.

After what felt like forever, with her entire body aching, Faye reached the Kebury's docks. Five medium-sized boats were anchored inside, swaying gently in the water's embrace. Faye also noticed several vessels a bit further away with corpses hung over the railings and bits of flesh floating on the rippling surface.

She looked over her shoulder at the gloomy streets, still pondering whether she should bother trying to escape when the malady was likely already festering inside her. Still, she eventually decided to push forward, unwilling to accept her demise, which seemed more imminent with every passing moment.

Faye checked three boats without success before finally finding the keys to the fourth one lying by the cockpit. She started the engine, then raised the anchor before sailing out of the dock into the vast sea.

The tall city buildings were getting further away as she peered into the rippling expansion soaked by the crimson illumination. Faye's eyelids were quickly becoming heavier. Exhausted, her flesh riddled with numerous aches, she leaned on the helm, trying desperately to keep herself from fading. But eventually, her mind drifted into the deep dark, and she felt her body crumbling on the deck.

After the shadows parted, Faye saw herself standing in the dark alley with the foreign woman's rotting corpse lying before her. The flesh was beginning to fall off her bones, and Faye could see white maggots feasting on her insides. Horrified, she took a step back, then turned and started running toward the street on the other side, but the faster she ran, the further it got from her. And soon, she was standing amidst the shadows with nothing but brick walls of tall apartment buildings outstretching in front and behind her.

Faye stopped, panting, sweat rolling down her face. She looked around, confused, unsure what to do next. Then, she noticed something moving in the distant dark. Faye squinted her eyes, trying to discern what it was. Then, several seconds later, she was struck with the horrible realization that the *thing* moving in the distance was a group of fish-headed abominations with scaly bodies and bulging black eyes.

Faye gasped, then turned and started rushing in the opposite direction, listening to the angry gargling behind her while taking heavy breaths. She ran for a couple minutes, then, just as the beastly bellows started becoming more distant, she saw six blue-skinned beings with pear-shaped heads in front of her. Their bodies were covered in animal pelts, and they were holding large spears in their bony hands.

The creatures started barking and growling, then lowered their weapons and began approaching. Terrified, Faye took a few steps back, then looked over her shoulder to see that fishmen were just fifty yards away, and she could already hear their webbed feet splashing on the rough ground. "No!" she whimpered. "Stay away! Just leave me alone!"

Faye pressed her back against the wall, covering her head with both hands. Then suddenly, following an eerie howl, the windows of the surrounding apartment buildings shattered, and hairy bodies of wolfmen started raining down, some landing just several yards away.

Faye shrieked in terror. Then, deciding to take her chances with the blue-skinned creatures, she lunged forward, but it was already too late. One of the wolfmen grabbed her and dragged her to the ground while gnawing on her shoulder, splattering hot blood everywhere. Seconds later, she felt the slimy hand of the fishman grabbing her by the leg, sinking its sharp nails into her flesh. Then finally, she saw the tall blue monster standing above her. It raised its spear, then brought it down, running it through Faye's heart as she screamed in fear and agony.

Just as she was about to fade into death's cold embrace, the scenery abruptly changed, and she found herself lying on the deck. Although the monsters were gone, the pain persisted, throbbing in every inch of her body. Faye moaned hoarsely, her hazy eyes shifting to the backpack beside her. In her mind arose images of the pouch filled with dark-blue powder.

If it's a drug, maybe I could use it to alleviate my suffering.

Faye extended her trembling hand, grabbed the bag, unzipped it, and pulled the pouch from inside. She looked at its contents briefly, then grabbed a handful and shoved it into her mouth.

Faye immediately started coughing and wheezing as the incredibly sour powder burned her dried-out throat. Bright lights momentarily flashed at the corner of her vision, and for a split second, she thought she was choking. But then, the burning sensation subsided, also lifting some of her bodily pains. Encouraged, Faye pushed off the ground, took another scoop, this time a bit smaller, and put it in her mouth. Again, she wrinkled her nose and gagged a few times, but the burning wasn't as bad as the first time.

Faye proceeded to have several more small scoops until her aches completely went away. Then, she returned the half-full pouch to the backpack, got up, and grabbed the helm, looking at the compass mounted beside it. "Pretty good stuff," she mumbled. "Maybe I'm going to make it to Talos after all."

She turned the helm and straightened the ship, then advanced the throttle, hearing the engine roar as she soared through the waves, the wind fluttering her short blonde hair. A faint smirk appeared on Faye's face, and all the memories of the terrible events she had to go through faded in the metallic bellow.

Suddenly, the horrific scream engulfed everything, shattering her momentary reverie. It was much louder than in the continent, and Faye could feel her eardrums vibrating painfully. She covered her ears with her hands, but it did little to stop the sound from digging into her consciousness, making her scream from pain and agitation.

The nightmare lasted for several seconds before the monstrous voice finally began to fade. Faye gasped a few times, then grabbed onto the helm to keep her balance before peering at the crimson waters again. What she saw made her body shudder violently as her mind quivered, teetering on the edge of lunacy.

From the depths of the sea emerged hundreds of gargantuan tentacles towering high into the sky. Thick and sinewy, they writhed with eerie grace, their slimy surface glistening under the crimson moonlight. Then, Faye heard an ominous growl, and with her widened eyes, she saw numerous maws opening on the flesh of these ghastly appendages, filled with sharp fangs biting incessantly at the air.

Whimpering and mumbling something that she herself couldn't comprehend, Faye grabbed the helm and turned it quickly, trying to escape the madness outstretching before her. But unfortunately, it was already too late.

Three tentacles sprang toward the boat and wrapped around it. Faye could hear the structure of the vessel creak tearfully, then, following a loud crack, she was submerged underwater, peering at hundreds of quivering limbs outstretching toward her from the dark depth.

In desperation, Faye grabbed the backpack slowly sinking beside her, pressed it to her body, and closed her eyes, waiting for the devil of the sea to drag her into the underworld where she would suffer eternally for all the sins she had committed during her self-serving existence.

Keri

They were driving through the city of Dahbus when suddenly, everything became shrouded by a thick mist. Darren slowed the truck, then glanced at Keri, who was looking at the road ahead. She could feel some being approaching them through the rippling of space caused by the vileness of its spirit. It was different from the rest of the beasts they had encountered along the way, which Keri easily defeated, using her newfound ability to release the emerald energy of the cosmos.

Although such actions used to inflict the continuous deterioration of her body, something had happened while she wandered the shadows of her past, helping the tortured souls reach their places of respite. Now, she could use the primal energy at will without causing any physical harm to her flesh. Nonetheless, Keri could feel that something was shifting within her, and she wondered whether there would be anything of her former self left in the aftermath of the final battle.

"There's something ahead of us," Darren uttered, then slowed the truck, peering into the distant murk. "Should I stop?"

Keri nodded, then turned toward the others huddled at the back. "Everyone, stay back. Let me handle this."

After the car stopped, Keri stepped out and took a few steps forward, breathing the cold air permeated with the stench of death. As she peered into the thick mist, trying to locate the source of the infernal energy, it parted, and out of it emerged Sila, clad in her black cloak, a predatory smirk gleaming on her face.

"So it was you," Keri spoke. "I wondered when you're going to show up again."

The witch chuckled, then turned her eyes to the people in the truck. "Well, come closer, everyone, don't be shy. Darren, Christa, Eliza, Kyron, Daniel, and precious little Nina. I want to give each of you your last opportunity to surrender and leave this world before you're swallowed by the Great Maw."

"Leave them out of this!" Keri exclaimed, taking a step closer. "This fight is between you and me."

"Far from it, my precious little sparkle," Sila said, then raised her eye patch to reveal an empty hole filled with emerald light. "This is the end of the road. It was fun playing with you all, but did you really expect me to let you thwart my master's vision?"

A series of bangs pierced the eerie tranquility, and three bullets soared through the air, aiming for Sila's head. However, the closer they got, the slower they became until they finally stopped completely and hung in space for a few seconds before shattering into tiny fragments.

Keri turned to see Eliza standing with a smoking pistol in her hand, her eyes wide with anger. Meanwhile, Sila chuckled once more, then brushed off a few strands of her blond hair falling on the gleaming hole in her face before continuing: "Did you honestly believe that it would work, darling? That anything would? Now kneel and accept your fate or suffer for eternity between the looms of time!"

Keri focused her attention on Sila again. "Stop your pointless blabber! I've had enough of your lies! It's time to end this."

The witch tilted her head to the side, the emerald gleam becoming brighter. "Oh sweet Keri – so eager to step into the shadow. Fine. Be it your way. Let's end this pointless struggle."

Sila raised her delicate hand and made a gripping motion. Moments later, the truck exploded in a cloud of blue dust, launching its passengers into the air.

"No!" Keri screamed, then lunged forward, but after taking only a few steps, she felt like she slammed into a brick wall.

She staggered backward, moaning in pain and anger. Meanwhile, Sila chuckled, summoning a line of sharp blue crystals that she flung with a swipe of her hand. Keri tried to dodge, but two of them pierced her shoulder, immediately freezing her flesh and numbing her senses.

Someone started shooting, but none of the bullets could breach the protective barrier. Sila cackled maniacally, then raised her hand, summoning a massive cloud in the sky that started raining down icicles, one of them slicing Keri's face open.

She wobbled, hearing someone scream behind her, but she didn't turn to look. Instead, she fixed her eyes on Sila and lunged forward, clawing with her remaining hand and biting at the barrier, feeling the ethereal energy pulsating within.

The witch smirked mockingly, then raised her arms, preparing to cast another spell when, following a loud screech, a crack appeared in the air. The expression on Sila's face changed, and Keri saw her eyebrows rise slightly. At that moment, Keri summoned every last bit of strength she had left and swung with her hand, screaming: "Shoot her! Shoot the damn hag!"

The barrier shattered. Seconds later, bullets started flying from two directions, piercing Sila's body and dropping her to the ground. Keri took a deep breath, then rushed forward, jumped on top of the witch, and, while looking into her eye, bit into her neck.

Briefly, everything disappeared. Then, a brilliant vista opened before Keri's eyes. She saw the cosmos and the countless worlds between. She

114

saw mages living in their giant castles and the ice giants wandering the desolate plains. Then, she saw a blue butterfly slowly flapping its wings before perching on the branch of a massive tree towering over the entire universe. As Keri continued to look, the back of the butterfly began to part, revealing a boundless abyss with a giant purple eye gleaming in the middle, radiating an ethereal presence as old as the universe itself.

Keri blinked, realizing she was kneeling on the street, holding a black cloak. She lingered for a bit, the voices of the Beyond still echoing at the back of her mind. Then, she got up and quickly turned, looking at the remnants of their truck lying amidst the street laden with pointy icicles that were quickly melting, forming glistening puddles underneath.

The first one she saw was Darren, leaning on the side of the building with a part of his face sagging awkwardly, seemingly from the broken jaw. Then, she heard someone rustling and looked to the opposite side of the street, where Eliza was slowly rising from the ground, shaken but unscathed.

"Is… everyone okay?" Keri asked.

She heard someone sobbing and stepped forward, squinting, trying to peer through the slowly fading mist. Soon the silhouettes emerged, and after getting closer, she saw Nina kneeling next to Christa's body. It was riddled with icicles, blood still seeping from numerous wounds, and her dead eyes wide open, staring into nowhere.

"Miss Christa saved me," the girl whimpered, tears rolling down her cheeks.

Keri looked into the girl's eyes, then turned, noticing something moving under the torn-off section of the truck's roof. She quickly approached to see Daniel trapped underneath, his face covered in blood and one of his ears drooping awkwardly, seemingly barely hanging on his head.

"Boss!" Darren yelled hoarsely, then rushed forward and, with some effort, raised the roof and threw it aside, allowing Daniel to get out.

"Where is Kyron?" Keri asked, looking around.

She heard a muffled gargle and saw the old man lying twenty yards away with a big piece of metal sticking out of his chest. Keri approached and knelt beside him, looking into his quickly fading eyes.

"Promise me you'll send that demon back to hell," Kyron uttered hoarsely. "Promise me you'll liberate my land and my people."

"I promise," Keri said, then watched as the life left the man's eyes. She then got up and turned to the surviving members of her crew.

Daniel was leaning on Darren's shoulder, Eliza was staring blankly into nowhere, and Nina was still sobbing, looking at Christa's corpse.

"We need to keep moving," Keri said.

Everyone stood silent, with a cold breeze blowing past them. Then, the eerie stillness was broken by another scream of the entity awaiting at sea.

"I'll go find us another car," Darren said after the monstrous voice grew quiet again.

The man helped Daniel to get up, then walked off. Meanwhile, Keri hobbled to Nina, knelt beside the girl, and hugged her tightly.

"I can feel *it* rising," Nina whimpered.

"I'm sorry I've brought this curse upon you, little one," Keri said. "You don't need to go with me." She raised her eyes, looking at Eliza and Daniel, then added: "None of you need to go with me."

"We already went through this," Daniel uttered.

"The lady in white told me not to leave your side," Nina said, looking at Keri with her glinty blue eyes.

"The lady in white…" Keri whispered, thinking about the ethereal gleam and the clanging of chains that guided her through the shadows. "I just hope she's still with us."

Eliza

Eliza sat in the back of an old sedan with Nina huddled next to her and Daniel on the other side, heaving and wheezing through his swollen mouth. Keri and Darren sat in front with the man's hands clutching the wheel and eyes fixed on quickly approaching buildings of Kebury Port.

Eliza's mind was filled with gloomy thoughts about all the people that succumbed to the infernal will. Despite the horrors they had experienced, she was still fearful of whatever awaited them at the sea. And that fear grew with every mile they got closer to the waters of Dilos, glistening in the crimson illumination as if containing all the blood spilled in this horrible battle.

They haven't encountered any more monsters in their journey from Dahbus, and the lands around them were drenched in eerie silence disturbed only by the occasional howl of the wind as if the world itself was lamenting its impending demise.

Can humanity really recover from this? Even if we somehow push back the cosmic malice, is it really worth it if no one is left to carry on?

Finally, they stopped by the docks, exited the car, and, for a while, stood in silence, looking at the four medium-sized boats swaying on the waves.

"We should take at least two," Eliza said. "That way, if one of them gets sunk, we won't get stranded in the middle of the sea."

"Good thinking," Daniel agreed, leaning on the side of their car. "Darren and I can take one boat while you three take the second."

"Sounds like a plan," Keri said, stepping onto the pier.

"Wait, there's someone over there!" Darren exclaimed, pointing at the sandy shoreline extending by the docks.

Eliza turned and squinted to see a person washed up on the beach. They quickly approached, soon realizing it was a woman with white hair clutching a backpack in her hands.

"She's still alive," Darren said after crouching beside her and checking the pulse. He then grabbed the woman by the shoulders and dragged her away from the smashing waves, propping her back against a large rock.

"She's one of the people who stole my things!" Keri exclaimed. "She had blonde hair back then, but I'm sure it's her." She leaned over, carefully pulled the backpack out of the woman's hands, unzipped it, and looked inside. "All the weapons are gone, but the flower powder is still there."

"Well, that's something at least," Daniel said, then turned his gaze to the unconscious woman. "What should we do with her?"

"We can't just leave her… right?" Eliza uttered.

"Well, we can't take her with us, so I don't see any other option," Keri said while swinging the backpack over her shoulder. "Unless one of you changed your mind and decided to stay behind."

She looked at the faces of her comrades, then turned and started ambling back to the docks with Nina, Darren, and Daniel following behind her. Eliza looked one last time at the woman, then sighed and joined them.

The group picked two boats standing next to each other. They found the keys of one of them hidden inside a large book in the storage compartment of the cockpit. Unfortunately, Darren had to hot-wire the second one, which took him almost ten minutes because his expertise was limited to cars. But eventually, they heard the roar of the engine and, after splitting their tiny crew, set out into the unknown.

Keri

The screams were now coming every couple of minutes, vibrating everything around. Nina was crying in the corner of the cockpit, and Eliza was trying to comfort her with little success. Keri looked at them while holding the helm with one hand, regretting not being more insistent on facing the Maw of the Hollow alone.

They already went through so much. There's little they can do against the beast, so why drag them to a definite peril? Even if we reign victorious, the chances of our survival seem bleak at best.

Keri winced as another scream came from the distance, making the ringing in her ears almost insufferable. She turned her head, looking at the second boat with Darren and Daniel swaying on the high waves a bit further away. Then, she fixed her eyes on the waters ahead.

"The beast is almost here," Keri said. "Eliza, could you take the helm?"

Her friend looked at her with fearful eyes, then nodded, got up, and took over while Keri increased the throttle before putting on the backpack and limping out of the cockpit.

"Where are you going?!" Eliza yelled through the roar of the engine.

"I'm going to face it head-on!"

Keri felt a light tug and lowered her eyes to see Nina standing beside her. "You take care of Eliza for me, okay?" Keri said, smiling faintly.

Nina pouted her lower lip, then nodded and took a step back. Keri gave her one last look, then turned and walked to the bow, peering at the crimson skies that grew darker by the minute.

This is it. Any moment now, I'll encounter the demon that has haunted my dreams since I saw its shadow in Exter.

She took one step closer and leaned on the railing, suddenly noticing something moving under the water. Keri's eyes widened, and her heartbeat quickened as dozens of giant writhing tentacles emerged from the depth and sprang toward their ship. She heard Eliza screaming and turned to see one of the slimy appendages wrapped around her friend's leg, trying to pull her overboard.

"Eliza!" Nina screamed, her eyes briefly turning bright green as a wave of energy washed over the monstrous limb, forcing it to let go of its prey.

Keri also heard screams coming from the distance, followed by rapid gunfire. She shifted her eyes to the second boat, now entangled by numerous slithering limbs. Gritting her teeth, she extended her hand forward while her eyes lit up with glistening emerald light.

The air around thickened, then, following a loud crackle, a beam of energy shot from her palm and soared high into the air before exploding into a myriad of smaller beams that wrapped around the two boats, pushing the quivering tentacles away.

More of the sinewy feelers rose from the wavering water, slamming at the barriers with increased ferocity, and Keri momentarily felt like the source of her otherworldly powers was slipping away. But then, she dug deeper by sinking her teeth into her lower lip, channeling all her resolve and anger, continuously repelling the attacks.

The beastly limbs tried for several more minutes, straining and contorting. Yet, all their attempts proved futile, and they eventually retreated back into the depth, leaving the two boats to sway in eerie tranquility.

Keri lowered her hand, dispelling the protective barriers, and crumbled to her knees, coughing and gagging with multicolored circles rippling before her eyes and every inch of her body burning as if her skin was about to peel off, exposing her battered flesh.

It seems I can only push my newfound abilities so far. It was naive to believe that my human body could hold such energy without eventually suffering the consequences.

"Keri!" she heard Eliza scream and turned to see the woman leaving the cockpit and stepping toward her.

"Go back to the helm!" Keri yelled.

"But—"

"Hurry! Before those things return."

Eliza gave her an intent look but didn't argue further – just went back to the cockpit and advanced the throttle, making their boat shoot forward. Keri glanced at Daniel and Darren, following close behind. She then turned her attention to the strange purple mist looming by the horizon. As they continued sailing at full speed, it enveloped everything, and they had to slow down, afraid of getting lost or hitting something in their path.

They sailed surrounded by complete silence for a while. Then, from a distance, came a sharp sound piercing the uneasy serenity. It was not the beastly scream but the toot of the horn. Seconds later, the mist parted, giving way to two massive cruise ships.

"Keri, what's going on?!" she heard Eliza's voice but didn't turn around, her attention fixed on the metallic monstrosities before them.

After the ships got closer, she saw hundreds of ghouls standing by the railing, their hollow eyes set on the two tiny boats sailing past them. They reminded her of creatures she encountered in the shadow of Atheta. But thankfully, they didn't have any weapons in their bony hands, and they didn't exhibit any hostile behavior. Instead, they only stared vacantly while standing motionless by the edge.

Keri breathed a sigh of relief after the ships passed, but that relief came with a grim brooding about the state of the world. She presumed that these might've been tourist ships caught amidst the sea when the chaos came, and all their passengers succumbed to the ghastly curse, damning them to wander the vast waters for the eternities to come. "Unless I put a stop to it," she mumbled.

As they proceeded, the air seemed to thicken, and the waves on the water's surface grew calmer, as if even the sea itself was holding its breath in anticipation of the upcoming confrontation that would determine the fate of the human race.

After a while, they heard distant shrieks, and soon, they saw numerous dark figures swarming the skies. Keri quickly realized that these were the same demons she had first encountered in Lynn. She then raised her hand, debating whether to unleash her energy and free them from their horrid curse. However, since they didn't seem eager to descend from their heavenly domain and attack them, she decided against it.

I need to save whatever strength I have left for the final confrontation.

The ranks of demons kept growing, seemingly thousands of them now soaring in the crimson skies, screeching and shrieking, celebrating the coming of their monstrous lord. Then, at the precipice of their infernal revelry, the beasts abruptly grew silent, and Keri felt some otherworldly presence crossing the point of no return and entering the world.

It started with a tiny ripple on the water's surface. Then, Keri noticed something moving about a mile away. Her eyes widened, and she felt her essence trembling, some part of her wishing to fall dead right at this moment so that she wouldn't have to face the malice that traveled billions of light-years, beckoned by the corruption of the world. Then, she heard the horrific scream that quickly grew in intensity, sending ripples through time and space as the beast of unfathomable horror emerged from the bowels of the sea.

It came in the form of a gargantuan amalgamation of malformed flesh and contorted limbs, at least five times the size of the creature she encountered at Exter. Its body rippled and shifted while countless black eyes peered at Keri, who stood at the bow, trying her hardest not to lose sanity in the face of the cosmic deity known to her as the Maw of the Hollow.

As the unholy writhing flesh covered the entire horizon, a hole appeared at its center, soon turning into a gaping mouth filled with razor-sharp fangs; inside it outstretched an inky abyss filled with countless smaller mouths, each biting incessantly, salivating in anticipation of the grisly feast.

Just like back in that horrific day, as soon as the maw of eldritch madness finished expanding, there was a brief flicker, followed by a humming screech. Then, Keri heard an ear-piercing whistle and soon saw a plethora of black lines soaring toward her. From the ends of those lines, tiny hands emerged, ready to grab her and drag her into the darkest night.

Keri pulled the pouch with the powder out of her backpack, then grabbed a handful and shoved it into her mouth. She chewed several times, then swallowed the sour substance, feeling every inch of her flesh throbbing with ethereal energy. Then, she took a deep breath and released a ferocious bellow, her eyes gleaming with bright emerald light that enveloped the two boats, forming a massive protective barrier. The black hands smashed into it, clawing and trying to push through. Meanwhile, Keri gritted her teeth, peering at the cosmic malice before her while reaching into the deepest parts of her essence while at the same time calling out to the powers that guided her so far.

My only shot is to concentrate whatever energy I have and release it all at once. My body will likely be disintegrated, but it will have to do. If what Sila said is true and I'm related to her in some bizarre way, it's probably for the betterment of this world for me to perish in this final fight.

Keri took another scoop of the powder and was about to unleash her final attack when from a distance came an echoey demonic voice speaking in the language she had never heard before: "Karkul zorathak, shal'khar ar'gath! Vorak'thar vazgor, shal'gul nak'rath!"

The reality shifted. The crimson illumination of the moon gave way to the purple gleam, and for a moment, Keri saw a giant eye peering at her from the Stygian abyss looming in the hellish maw. Then, she felt something breaking inside her, and she crumbled to her knees, shackled by the cosmic presence of something beyond the grasp of her feeble mind.

The emerald barrier dispersed, allowing the hands to get through. Soon, she heard Nina scream and felt a faint flicker of her energy in the girl's futile attempt to push away the ghastly limbs. Keri gasped a few times and tried to get up, but she was immediately entangled by the quivering black lines before being lifted into the air and carried toward the gnashing abyss.

Keri shrieked and sank her teeth into the darkness, but nothing happened; the power within her was silent, and instead of being transported into another realm, she saw herself being dragged closer and closer to her ultimate demise. Her eyes widened, and panic started to set in as she kept gnawing at the infernal limbs, feeling her teeth chipping and breaking. But unfortunately, her powers seemed to have abandoned her at the moment when she needed them the most.

Keri shrieked in desperation, the beastly maw now only fifty yards away. Then, just as she was about to disappear inside the chattering madness, a bright white light flickered at the corner of her eye, and reality shifted once more.

Keri felt herself falling through the layers of time before dropping heavily onto the white marble floor. She pushed off and got up, realizing she had both arms again. She then looked around the massive hall enveloped by an eerie silence. There were Gothic columns standing at least a hundred feet tall, holding a glistening white dome, while in the back loomed giant doors adorned with carvings of strange geometrical shapes pulsating with foreboding energy.

Keri took a deep breath, trying to recover from the terror still shrouding her mind while at the same time peering warily at the enormous structures surrounding her, trying her hardest to make sense of the transpiring events.

Were my encounters with Sila and the Maw even real, or were they just another test devised by the powers of Beyond? Or is this some form of an afterlife where I was transported after being swallowed by the beast?

Hesitantly, Keri started walking forward, her footsteps echoing eerily in the vastness of the hall. As she approached, the doors began to open, producing a muffled rustle. What appeared behind them made Keri stop, her eyes widening in fearful awe.

On the other side outstretched a narrow pathway, crossing a black void and leading to a colossal throne, which seemed to be carved out of a single block of black marble, every inch intricately detailed with strange shapes and symbols. Some of them were vaguely reminiscent of serpents, while others depicted beings Keri had never seen before. It was embellished with multicolored gemstones, carefully embedded to form patterns emanating a pallid glow.

On the throne sat a giantess dressed in flowing white robes, her pale skin glistening in the surrounding dark. She was shackled by numerous chains that coiled tightly around her, imprisoning her divine essence. Her eyes and a part of her face were concealed by a large blindfold that seemed to be woven out of the finest silk.

As Keri continued to peer fearfully, the being leaned forward, the chains holding her body producing tearful clangs that sent shivers down Keri's spine as she realized that this must be the entity that guided her through some of the darkest moments in her battle against the eldritch beasts.

"Welcome, Keri," the giantess spoke in a soft ethereal voice, permeating everything with soothing but, at the same time, ominous vibrations. "I'm pleased to finally meet you. I am Themis, known to many as the Lady of Light."

"What is happening?" Keri asked, her voice trembling, along with her body, as she stood before what she presumed to be one of the Ancients of the primordial universe. "Did you bring me here?"

"Yes and no. I heard your spirit shrieking amidst the darkest night, and I merely answered the call."

"Why me? Why not countless others who fell in this senseless battle?"

The corners of Themis's pale lips rose slightly. "I think you already know why."

"Is it because I was born from Sila's shining?"

Themis didn't answer – just continued smiling faintly.

"What happens now?" Keri asked.

"Now it's time to choose – submit your spirit to me, become the herald of the light, and continue your valiant struggle, or perish in the insatiable maw, along with the rest of your realm."

"Doesn't seem like a choice to me," Keri said, lowering her eyes, initial awe now dwindling and giving way to feelings of hope but also frustration. She stood silent for a bit, then raised her head to Themis again. "Why are the Ancients doing this? Why did Sila invade my world and open the gates for the beast? Why did Leviathan, Heket, Fenrir, and the Corpse Crawler choose our world as their wicked playground?"

"You have many questions, yet your time dwindles," Themis spoke, leaning back in her throne, the clanging of chains resonating throughout the void. "Should you choose to enter my service, perhaps one day, the truth will be revealed to you. However, I can not lift the veil at this instant since your spirit already teeters on the precipice of fracture, and such enlightenment might rend it to dust.

"So choose, Keri, to accept or to refuse. Just know that all I'm offering is a chance – even with the power I'm willing to bestow upon thee, you may fall in the battle against the combined might of the God of Chaos and the Maw of the Hollow. And should that be the case, you would be left alone, wandering the cosmos as my loyal servant, knowing that your world had been eradicated by the Great Devourer."

"I accept," Keri said firmly. "If my world falls, it matters not to me what happens to my spirit."

"Sublime," Themis said, seemingly pleased, while raising her right hand. "I never before had a Struggler in my service and expect great things to come from our divine accord."

124

From Themis's palm came a beam of dazzling white light that shot right through Keri, filling her with pulsating cosmic energy. For a moment, billions of images flashed before her eyes of aeons spent watching the universe from the heavenly domain that the Lady of Light created, shielding herself from entropy that could cause a deterioration of her ancient spirit. She also saw countless other beings who served or were still serving Themis, some resembling humans while others seemed closer to the beasts she tried to defeat. Then, she felt herself falling through the void, moving toward the madness residing in her realm.

Keri saw the gnashing abyss and the Eye of Chaos peering at her intently. She screamed, releasing the ethereal energy endowed by Themis, its white luminescence mixing with the emerald gleam coming from her eyes. The black hands loosened their grip and retracted, and she heard an angry hiss, followed by a ferocious roar that flung her backward, trembling her very essence.

Just before falling into the purple sea, Keri raised her hand to the sky, summoning a white dome that surrounded her and the two ships. Then, she rose into the air, looking intently at the plethora of black eyes rippling on the abomination's body.

Now or never.

Keri bit her lower lip as hard as she could. For a few seconds, her heart stopped. Then, from her chest erupted a massive emerald beam that soared through the sky before slamming into the unholy amalgamation of quivering madness, piercing through it while raising flesh, guts, limbs, and some thick black mass into the air.

The creature screeched horribly. Seconds later, the purple light faded, giving way to the illumination of the blood moon as the Eye of Chaos retreated into the black abyss. Encouraged, Keri soared closer to the injured beast before summoning another beam from her chest, aiming it right in the middle of the ghastly maw.

Everything trembled, and the monstrous figure flickered before producing another sickening screech.

"Go back into the void!" Keri screamed. "And take your infernal spawns with you!"

Gritting her teeth, ignoring the painful fluttering of her heart, she prepared to release the third beam, intending to finish the creature even if it meant her own demise. But then, something changed, and she felt shivers running down her spine, accompanied by a feeling that something horrible was about to happen.

The gargantuan monstrosity released a tearful shriek as its massive body started shaking and contorting, some of its limbs and eyes detaching from the flesh and falling into the rippling waters. Then, from the inky abyss erupted a torrent of blood, splashing Keri from head to toe. Moments later, from the deepest pits of hell emerged a massive demonic hand glowing with fiery red. Its skin was textured with jagged scars etched deep into the flesh and smoldering with fading embers. The beastly claw grabbed onto the side of the maw, digging deep with its sharp nails. Then, from the hollow appeared a giant head with twisted, gnarled horns protruding from the top of its exposed skull.

The demon opened its mouth, baring its sharp fangs, and released a horrific cacophony that sounded like thousands of anguished spirits shrieking in unison. Then, it fixed its bulging black eyes on Keri before leaping into the world, exposing its giant frame and broad flaming wings.

Keri's mind was screaming out of sheer terror as her sanity finally gave out, all the coherent thoughts she still had giving way to the horrific images of the vast universe ruled by the malicious ancient deities who wanted nothing else than to debauch and devour everything that was living. Yet, there was still a tiny part inside her that wanted to continue struggling to the very end, and at this moment, that relentless inner determination took over her wailing essence.

Keri screamed before conjuring another beam, aiming it at the demon's head. However, the beast easily dodged out of the way before raising its claw and swiping at Keri, breaking her protective barrier and smashing her into the rippling sea.

She felt her chest tightening and an intense pain radiating through her torso, shackling her limbs, as she started sinking into the frigid sea. Keri gasped and felt water rushing into her lungs. Meanwhile, her fading sight caught a glimpse of the demon extending its claw and grabbing Eliza's and Nina's boat.

Keri felt the girl's fear, and for a second, she peered through her eyes at the grotesque demon opening its mouth, intending to swallow the boat whole along with its two passengers. Eliza was firing her pistol, and shots were also coming from the second boat, but the bullets couldn't even break the beast's hardened skin.

As the vision faded, Keri felt herself sinking into the darkness, leaving everything behind. With her last effort, she extended her hand, summoning one final train of thought – a call for help that she sent into the cosmos.

Please. I'll do whatever you want. I'll serve you until the end of time. Just give me one last chance. To fight back against the evil that is about to destroy my world.

Everything stopped. Somewhere very far away, a blindfold slid from Themis's face. Then, an eye opened, filled with bright white light that lit

126

up the entire universe.

Keri felt ethereal energy surging through her body, lifting her out of the water in a single burst. She soared into the sky, again coming face to face with the demon and the Maw of the Hollow wavering behind him. In her mind, she heard Themis's soft whisper. Then, from the stump where her right hand used to be, erupted thousands of glistening white chains. They flew toward her otherworldly foes and wrapped around their flesh.

The horned demon bellowed horribly, releasing its grip on the boat, which dropped into the water and fractured in half. Breathing heavily, Keri grabbed onto the heavenly chains, still feeling Themis's might pulsating through her. Then, she pulled with whatever strength she had left, shattering the cosmic entities before her into billions of tiny pieces.

Faye

Faye gasped and opened her eyes, then started coughing frantically. Wheezing, she pushed off the sandy shore, then looked around to see remnants of her boat floating on the gentle waves. She spent some time looking for injuries on her body, then frowned, trying desperately to remember what had happened.

She recalled falling asleep on the boat and having a horrible nightmare about beasts trying to tear her apart. What occurred after was mostly a blur, and Faye decided not to push it after catching a momentary glimpse of some ghastly limbs writhing at the edge of her consciousness.

Suddenly, her eyes widened as she realized that instead of being drenched in crimson, the shoreline was basking in the warming rays of the sun, hanging high in the blue sky. Stumped, Faye turned her head to the vast waters of the sea and saw a giant white mushroom cloud glistening by the horizon. She lingered for some time, then started hobbling to the nearby docks, wincing every few steps. Although her injuries inflicted by Sofia and Julie seem to have healed, there was still tightness in her chest accompanied by a throbbing pain in her head.

After reaching the docks, Faye saw two boats standing inside. She started limping toward one of them, then turned, widening her eyes after seeing several dozen figures shambling on the beach. Her heart began to pound, thinking she was about to be ambushed by monsters again, but as she looked closer, she realized that those were people. They seemed disoriented, shambling around aimlessly, their bodies naked or covered in rags. Yet, they didn't show any signs of beastly corruption.

Faye hesitated, then glanced at the bright sun before leaving the docks and stepping onto the beach. Then, she raised her hand and called out hoarsely: "Hey! Are you guys okay?!"

Eliza

"We need to keep looking!" Eliza exclaimed tearfully, her eyes fixed on the surrounding white mist.

Darren and Daniel shared glances with one another but remained silent. Feeling desperate, Eliza turned to Nina, sitting on the bow, wrapped in a ragged blanket, shivering, her hair still wet from the plunge they took into the cold waters of the sea after their boat broke apart.

"Nina, you need to help us find her," Eliza said, crouching beside the girl.

"I can't feel her anymore," Nina whimpered. "I also no longer see the pretty green light when I close my eyes."

Eliza rubbed her nose, then returned to the railing, looking intently at the water's murky surface.

"The sun is setting," she heard Daniel's voice.

Her heart fluttered painfully, and she looked over her shoulder before uttering: "Are you really willing to give up on her so easily? Despite everything she has done for us? Despite everything she has done for this world?"

"It has already been hours," Darren said grimly, lowering his eyes to the deck. "No way could she survive that long in this freezing water."

"This is Keri you're talking about!" Eliza shouted. "She survived her arm being bitten off by the infernal wolf and still had enough strength left to slay the beast."

An uneasy silence descended onto the boat, disturbed only by the soft grumbling of the outboard motor.

"Let's search until it gets dark, okay?" Eliza said. "Then, we can decide what to do next."

Daniel looked into her eyes, then gave her a short nod. Meanwhile, Darren turned the helm, and they continued circling the area where they confronted the Maw of the Hollow, now covered with white mist, which was beginning to dissipate, allowing the rays of the setting sun to push through.

With the light quickly fading, Eliza peered at the surrounding waters, her heart beating more and more heavily in her chest. She knew she should be happy that the demons were pushed back and the world was potentially saved from corruption. But at this moment, these things mattered not in the prospect of losing her best friend, feelings for whom continued to flourish in her heart.

The sun was beginning to sink into the vast expansion of the sea, and with the coming darkness, Eliza's eyes began to well with tears. She was about to crumble to the deck and start weeping when she noticed two broken-off planks floating on the rippling surface with a person lying on top of them.

"Over there!" Eliza hollered, pointing with her finger, her eyes wide and her heart pounding like crazy in her chest.

It took them several minutes to reach Keri and pull her into the boat. Eliza embraced her friend's frigid body, looking at her ashen face and blue lips. "Keri?" she whimpered. "Keri, please wake up."

"I feel a pulse, but it's very weak," Darren said, crouching beside them.

"We need to get her back to Orox!" Eliza exclaimed, pulling Keri closer.

Darren nodded, then went back into the cockpit, turned the boat, and started speeding across the rising waves. Meanwhile, Eliza continued cradling her friend while whispering: "Please don't leave me, Keri. I have no one else. Even if the world is saved, I don't know if I could continue without you."

She noticed a slight tremble of Keri's eyelids, and the woman's lips parted slightly before releasing a faint wheeze.

"Keri, please," Eliza continued begging tearfully, her words muffled by the roaring of the engine as they sailed at full throttle, enveloped by the twilight of the upcoming night.

Keri

The cold wind was blowing, fluttering Keri's black hair. She sat on the balcony of a small lodge on the outskirts of Pirn, the small town in the eastern part of Orox, where she and Eliza chose to take respite in the aftermath of the battle.

Keri gazed vacantly at the vast meadows and the Kalenburg peaks glinting on the horizon. Despite their victory, her thoughts in the days after she woke up in a hospital bed in Dahbus were nothing but gloomy.

The battle was won for the world but not for me. It feels like big chunks were ripped out of my spirit, and I don't see myself ever being able to recover, knowing what lurks between the cosmos.

I wish for nothing else than to move on and start serving Themis under the promise I made. I can't help but think that I was, in a way, responsible for everything that had happened, that Sila chose this world partly because she was interested in turning me into one of her minions. While she spoke mostly in half-truths, I feel very strongly that, in this case, she wasn't lying. That my existence is somehow connected to her wicked gleam. Thus, as long as I remain in this world, the same could happen again.

I only still linger because of Eliza and the affinity that she feels toward me. I can't leave until I make her understand that no matter how much I'd like to indulge in the pleasantries of suburban life, it's just not going to happen. I must convince her to move on without me because otherwise, she would be sure to succumb to the allure of drugs and alcohol and waste away in the slums. I owe her this much.

"Keri?"

She turned slowly to see Eliza's head peeking through the doorway.

"Look what came to see us," Eliza said happily, then stepped aside.

Nina hopped into the balcony, then rushed toward Keri and hugged her tightly. "Hello, Miss Keri!" she chirped.

"Hello, Nina," Keri said while tousling the girl's curly hair. "Are you being a good girl?"

"She is," Daniel said, stepping from inside the room. He gave Keri a nod, then leaned toward Nina. "Go help Aunt Eliza set up the table. Me and Keri need to have a little talk."

The girl smiled happily, then rushed out of the balcony. Meanwhile, Daniel leaned on the railing, looking at the wondrous vista outstretching before them. He lingered briefly, then took a deep breath and spoke again: "So, how are you doing, Keri?"

"I'm okay," she said, mustering a smile. "Still trying to get acclimated to the new town."

"You know, the offer still stands for you two to come live in the palace. The repairs are almost complete, and both Nina and I would love to have you."

"Thanks. I'll keep it in mind."

The two fell silent. Keri gave a man a short glance. Seeing blue bags under his eyes, she wondered whether he was still haunted by the Corpse Crawler's voice and the glimpses of its infernal realm.

"So, how are things in the world?" she asked after a short pause.

Daniel sighed. "The things are rough. Yet, we had no more of the beastly sightings, so it's probably safe to assume that all the turned people had regained their human form. Although most don't remember anything, the surviving government officials are trying to control the narrative, saying that everything was caused by the biological weapon used by the terrorist organization that had since been eradicated by the Intercontinental Army. However, various rumors are going around, fueling numerous anti-government movements, which we'll need to take care of before the world can move on."

"Do they have a death toll yet?" Keri asked, her voice trembling slightly.

"No. But it's safe to say that at least half of Orox was wiped out. The situation is a lot better in Talos, but we're still talking about decades of rebuilding and restructuring before we can return to some level of normalcy."

"I see."

"Still, I believe strongly that we'll eventually recover, and it's only because of you, Keri, that we have this chance – don't you ever forget it."

The man squeezed her shoulder gently, then returned to the room. Meanwhile, Keri shifted her gaze to the distant mountains and was about to drift back into her grim brooding when she noticed a blue-winged butterfly perched on the railing.

A shiver ran down her spine, her eyes widened, and her heart started pounding in her chest as she looked at the broad wings slowly moving up and down. She expected any moment for the spine of the insect to part, revealing an Eye of Chaos peering from the inky abyss.

"The dinner is ready!" Eliza's soft voice called out.

Keri flinched and looked over her shoulder before returning to the railing, but the butterfly was already gone. She lingered for a little while, trying to calm her racing heart. Then, she grasped the rim of her wheelchair with her remaining hand, turned, and rolled inside, trying to ignore the cold wind blowing at her back, carrying an eerie chuckle.

Beckoned by the infernal will,
She stepped into the demon's nest,
And although the witch was slain,
The corruption continued to infest.

It followed her into the city,
Where it festered in the shadows deep,
And while the Queen showed no pity,
Her hold, in the end, proved meek.

Although the hero's heart was heavy,
Her eyes retained their gleam,
And even when the hunter had fallen,
She silenced the hag's scream.

She slew the monstrous eel,
And sailed across the sea,
To seize the howling mountain,
From the devil named Fenrir.

Although her flesh was broken,
She rose for the final fray,
And made the vow to Themis,
In the face of the end of days.

And now she sits on the throne of thorns,
Awaiting her destiny's call,
While the eldritch beasts of the cosmos,
Prowl the Eternal Halls.

Thank you so much for reading!

I hope you enjoyed the book. If you did, please take a minute to rate and share your review on Amazon. Writing means everything to me, and reader feedback helps me improve and reach a wider audience, contributing to my dream of writing full-time.

Find out more about my work!

Website: https://www.primaryhollow.com
Facebook: https://www.facebook.com/PrimaryHollow/
Instagram: https://www.instagram.com/primaryhollow/
Twitter: https://twitter.com/PrimaryHollow
Patreon: https://www.patreon.com/primaryhollow

Printed in Great Britain
by Amazon

23454362R00078